"She needs people to reach out to."

Clay's thoughtful eyes rested on Sheena. "Vicky needs a diversion, I'll agree with you there. And I'm hoping that between us we can provide one."

Her eyes met his. "We can try," she replied quietly.

"Good!" he said with evident satisfaction. "I was hoping you'd feel that way. First I suggest we get to know each other a little better. Then the news of our engagement won't seem a play to break down Vicky's defenses."

Sheena swallowed hard. "I don't think I can promise you that much support!" she said in an unnatural voice. "For goodness' sake, where did you get such an absurd idea?"

Clay's eyes went over her slight figure in a slow, appraising manner, and Sheena wanted to slap his arrogant face.

OTHER
Harlequin Romances
by JANE CORRIE

Many of these titles are available at your local bookseller.

For a free catalogue listing all available Harlequin Romances, send your name and address to:

HARLEQUIN READER SERVICE,
M.P.O. Box 707, Niagara Falls, N.Y. 14302
Canadian address: Stratford, Ontario, Canada N5A 6W2

The Station Boss

by

JANE CORRIE

Harlequin Books

TORONTO • LONDON • LOS ANGELES • AMSTERDAM
SYDNEY • HAMBURG • PARIS • STOCKHOLM • ATHENS • TOKYO

Original hardcover edition published in 1980
by Mills & Boon Limited

ISBN 0-373-02365-0

Harlequin edition published November 1980

Printed in U.S.A.

CHAPTER ONE

'SOMEONE to see you, Sheena,' said Mrs Rider, known as 'Cookie' to the inhabitants of Barter's Ridge, a prosperous sheep station in New South Wales.

'Me?' queried Sheena in a wondering voice as she flicked the last speck of dust off the redwood dresser and turned to face Cookie. 'You're sure they asked for me, and not Mrs Charter?'

Cookie gave an emphatic nod. 'It's you he particularly asked to see. He looks like a Ranger to me,' she added gently. 'Not that he's dressed as one, but there's something about those fellows,' she shrugged her ample form, 'well, you know what I mean.'

Sheena's hand holding the duster clenched round it, and her lovely sapphire blue eyes took on a bleak look. It could only mean one thing, they had found her father.

'Want me to come with you?' asked Cookie, not liking the pallor that now tinged Sheena's cheeks. 'I've put him in Doyle's study.'

Sheena drew a deep breath and shook her head, making the blue-black waves that framed her heart-shaped face spring away from her small features. 'No, thank you, Cookie,' she replied slowly, 'I'd rather be on my own,' then as a thought came to her she asked breathlessly, 'Is Doyle——?'

Cookie shook her head. 'He's not back from Sydney yet. I guess he's got held up somewhere. He shouldn't be long, though,' she replied.

Sheena nodded, then smoothed her dress down in a manner that suggested that she was trying to stall for time. Then she lifted up her head in a gesture that said, 'Let's get it over with,' and made her way to the study at the rear of the homestead.

The man stood by the study window gazing out at the wide expanse of green paddocks, visible from this side of the homestead. Sheena had an impression of height and authority and understood what Cookie had meant when she had said that she thought he was a Ranger.

When he turned to face her, the impression was still there—at least the authority was, but for some reason she couldn't explain, she didn't think he was a man of the law.

He was dressed much as any outrider would dress, but his clothes were good and fitted his tall frame as a second skin. The sort of good cloth that Doyle would wear, and this thought made her swallow quickly. 'I believe you asked to see me,' she said in a soft hesitant voice, as the thought went through her mind that that was about all that this man would have in common with Doyle, for Doyle was fair, whereas this man was dark, with dark forbidding brows, and even more forbidding black eyes that seemed to sear right through you, as they were doing now, she thought, as she waited for him to speak.

'Miss Greig?' he asked with a hint of a Northern

drawl, and at her swift nod continued, 'I'm Clay Day-man. You wouldn't have heard of me, but I've brought this as an introduction.' He slipped a lean hand into his leather waistcoat and produced something that he gave to her.

Sheena stared at the gold watch that she held in her hand. It was her father's, and her heart lurched painfully. 'He's dead, isn't he?' she said tonelessly, still looking at the watch.

The man gave a curt nod in answer to this. 'I would have come sooner,' he said, 'only I was away at some cattle sales in Wingham when it happened. I've a spread in Bellingen. Your father worked for me for the past two years.'

Sheena looked quickly away from the watch in her hand. Why had he to work? she asked herself bitterly. Surely the money he had stolen from Doyle would have been enough to keep him in comfort for the rest of his life?

She glanced swiftly at the man who was now staring down at the floor. Did he know that her father was a thief? she wondered.

His next words proved that he did. 'The payroll's there,' he said quietly. 'He told me where to find it. He'd cached it away on his trek to the North.'

He directed Sheena's attention to a well-worn saddlebag that lay on a chair opposite Doyle's desk. Sheena's lips firmed. She recognised the saddlebag, too. She wanted to weep her heart out, for in that bag lay the cause of all her unhappiness, and it hadn't even been spent. At least the thought of her father living in luxury had been some consolation for the shame and misery that she had endured for the past three years, and although that hadn't been the right way to look at it, there had been no other consolation for her.

'There's a letter,' Clay Dayman said, and felt in the top pocket of his blue checked shirt and took out a square envelope which he handed to her. 'He left me a note, that's how I knew about that,' his glance strayed towards the saddlebag and then back to her.

Sheena still stood there, one small hand clutching the letter and the other her father's watch. She was grateful for the man's kindness in carrying out her father's wishes, but now she wanted to be left alone. Her glance fell on the saddlebag. If this was a fairy story, the return of the stolen money should have made things come right for her, but it wasn't a fairy story, and it was too late for her dreams to come true, she thought bitterly.

'I'm very grateful for the trouble you've taken, Mr Dayman,' she said quietly. 'Have you come far this morning? Can I offer you some refreshment?' she asked.

Clay Dayman smiled, and it transformed his hard features. 'Not far for me, only a matter of fifty miles or so, and I won't trouble you to produce anything in the refreshment line. I'm returning up North to-morrow. If you've a mind to do as your father suggests,' his black eyes fell on the letter still unopened in her hand, 'then I'll be happy to escort you back to Bellingen with me.'

Sheena's sapphire blue eyes opened wide at this calm statement of his. Take her back to Bellingen with him—but why? For what?

'I think if you just read the letter,' Clay Dayman suggested gently.

Sheena swallowed. Then she blinked hard and started to open the letter. As she did so, Clay Dayman turned back to his perusal of the paddocks from out of the study window.

It wasn't a very long letter, but long enough for James Greig to say what he wanted to say. He asked Sheena to forgive him and to forgive the fact that he hadn't had the courage to return the money to Doyle. He had thought that her future was assured, and had only recently learned the truth by making some enquiries into her circumstances. 'I never thought that Doyle Charter would have gone back on his word. I swear that I would have returned and taken punishment for my blind and stupid mistake in taking that money, had I known the truth. Cut loose, girl; by what I've heard you've paid for your board and lodging there long enough. I've put Clay into the picture, and he's a man you can trust. I've a smallholding of sorts on the outskirts of his station, and a bit put by to keep you going until you get settled.'

Sheena's hand holding the letter fell slowly to her side. It had all looked so easy from his point of view, she thought numbly. He had forgotten one salient fact; she loved Doyle, and she would always love him. He hadn't broken the engagement, she had. The fact that he hadn't tried to talk her out of her decision was understandable. The Charters were an old and well respected family, and it had caused quite a stir in the high society to which they belonged when Doyle had courted his manager's daughter.

She could still remember with bitter clarity the wonderful moment when he had put that large glittering diamond ring on her third finger and asked her to marry him. She could still feel the pride she had felt at that moment, for Doyle was the most sought-after bachelor in the district, and his financial circumstances made him even more of a prize. Not that Sheena had thought of him that way. To her, he was Prince Charming, and she had adored him for years. She had been just fifteen when her father had started to work for Doyle's father, and subsequently for Doyle on his father's death. It was on her eighteenth birthday that Doyle had proposed to her.

This memory awakened others, and she was back again in the home that she had shared with her father. He had lost his wife, Sheena's mother, shortly before their move to New South Wales, after an operation that she had never recovered from, but he had carried on with the move, considering that it was better for both of them to start afresh elsewhere without the heartbreaking pull of old memories constantly around them.

Having applied for the position of manager at Barter's Ridge and being successful, Sheena's father was assigned quarters on the station, and Sheena found herself in the middle of the hustle of a thriving sheep station.

She had been happy, she thought wistfully, but never more so than that evening when she had proudly held her hand out to her father so that he could admire the ring. She recalled his words that had sounded so odd at the time. 'So you're safe now,' that was all that he had said. The next morning he left Barter's Ridge, and with him went the payroll, the station's largest pay-out for the year, for it was shearing time.

Sheena had returned Doyle's ring that same day. He had taken it and said harshly, 'Do you know what you're doing?' That was all that he had said. There had been no plea for her to reconsider, no assurance that naturally she was shocked and so was he, but he wasn't going to let her go, she couldn't be held responsible for what her father had done. All these words could have been said, but they weren't.

In the midst of her misery and shame for her father's action, the message had slowly seeped through to her that the words would never be said. Doyle was an important man, and his family too well-respected to even consider marrying a thief's daughter. Even Sheena's beauty could not compensate for this, and her pride would not allow her to forget it.

When Doyle had offered her the post of companion to his mother, she had accepted without reservation because he was also offering her somewhere to live. The quarters she had shared with her father would now house the new manager and there was nowhere else for Sheena to go. She had no other living relations, and no money. Doyle could have asked her to leave the station, but he hadn't and Sheena had felt a spark of hope that perhaps in time the past would be forgotten and he would ask her to marry him again.

She took a deep breath. That had been three years ago, and although Doyle treated her as one of the family, he had deliberately refrained from making any affectionate approaches to her. It was as if their love had never been, and if he had once loved her, then he had had second thoughts since, and it was now a thing of the past. As time slipped by, her post of companion to Mrs Charter had widened its boundaries, and she became a general factotum in the household chores, helping out wherever necessary and never complaining. The salary that she had been forced to accept was the minimum payable, and she would not have heard of accepting a higher one. In her eyes, she was lucky to have a roof over her head and three meals a day. She could never repay the money that had been taken, but she owed the family her living, and this was the only way that she could show her gratitude.

When the engagement between Doyle and Sheena had been ended, Doyle's mother had become distinctly friendlier towards her. There was no doubting the fact that she had felt that her handsome son could have made a better marriage, and she had had several suitable girls in mind; all came of wealthy families and were in close touch with the Charters. Her evident relief at Sheena's removal from the marital front was shown by her rather gushing efforts to make her feel wanted—to Sheena it was as if she was saying, 'Thank you' fervently each time they were alone together, but Sheena refused to dwell too much on this.

Her dreams of marrying Doyle remained dreams, as did the longing for him to take her in his arms again and kiss her as he had once done. Only the fact that she was near him and saw him each day compensated for her heartache. She found herself always looking for some little action on his part to show her that he still cared for her, but if his gaze did linger on her for a little longer than was necessary, he was careful to turn the conversation on to more general subjects, thus squashing any wishful thinking on her part.

'Well?' said the deep voice of Clay Dayman, and Sheena looked towards him, now facing her.

She swallowed. Sense told her that she ought to do what her father suggested, to cut loose, as he had put it, but leave tomorrow—— 'It doesn't give me much time, does it?' she said hesitantly.

'Time enough,' he answered firmly, his dark eyes noting the pallor of her cheeks. 'I'd say you've played your part,' he added, gazing at her significantly. 'Wouldn't you?'

'Can't you give me a little more time to think things over?' she asked, and swallowed. 'I can't just walk out on them like that.' She looked away from his searching eyes. 'I'm not even sure that I want to.'

'Well, that's up to you,' he replied slowly. 'But I'd say your father was right. Only there's a little more to it, isn't there?'

Sheena's pallor turned to a pink hue. He was talk-

ing about Doyle, and the real reason why she didn't
want to leave. Her soft lips firmed. It was no business
of his. If she wanted to stay at Barter's Ridge then
she would stay.

She was just about to voice these sentiments when
the study door opened and Doyle strode into the
room. His light blue eyes rested first on Sheena, then
on the tall figure of Clay Dayman, and back again to
Sheena. 'Company?' he said to her.

Sheena was about to make the introduction when
Clay Dayman took the initiative away from her by
walking forward and holding out a hard hand to
Doyle. 'Clay Dayman,' he said crisply. 'If you're
the owner of Barter's Ridge, then I guess this is your
property.' He walked over to where the saddlebag lay
and handed it to Doyle.

Doyle stared at the saddlebag, then he looked at
Sheena, who gave a dull nod. 'It's the payroll, Doyle,'
she said simply. 'Father never spent it.' She looked at
Clay. 'He's dead now, and he left Mr Dayman a
letter asking him to return it. He worked for Mr
Dayman.'

She said nothing about the letter her father had
left for her in which he had suggested that she go
back North with Clay Dayman.

Doyle's lips thinned as he said caustically, 'Better
late than never, I suppose,' and inclined his head towards the bag. 'There's a tidy sum in there, Dayman.
Are you claiming a percentage for the return?'

Sheena gasped. How could Doyle have said that!
There had been no trace of gratitude in his voice at

all. He must have made Clay Dayman feel like a bounty-hunter. 'Doyle!' she exclaimed hastily. 'I'm sure...'

Doyle's growled, 'Keep out of this Sheena,' prevented her from finishing the sentence.

'No percentage, Mr Charter,' answered Clay Dayman, with emphasis on the 'Mr'. 'James Greig asked a favour of me, and I'm doing my level best to fulfil it.' He turned his dark sardonic eyes on the embarrassed Sheena. 'Part of that favour was to take his daughter back up North with me. He'd saved up a fair amount to keep her going until she gets the smallholding he's left her up to scratch. I'm sorry she couldn't give you more notice that she's leaving. We're heading North tomorrow.'

Sheena blinked in disbelief. Her wide sapphire blue eyes stared at Clay Dayman. Why had he said that? He knew very well that she had been about to turn down her father's suggestion.

'Is this true, Sheena?' Doyle asked, rounding on her aggressively, almost daring her to say yes.

Sheena swallowed. She wanted to say no, that of course she wouldn't do a thing like that, but Clay Dayman's eyes were upon her, and no matter what she wanted to do she found herself unable to let him down. The words were out before she could recall them. 'I'm sorry, Doyle, but I think it would be for the best.' Her eyes pleaded with him to understand that things couldn't go on as they had, that she had had enough.

Once the words were out, she felt a sense of freedom flow over her. She ought to have done this a long time ago, or at least have made some effort to get away from Doyle's constant presence. A little voice inside her told her that if Doyle really loved her now was the time for him to prove it to her. Her worried eyes left Doyle's furious ones and she looked at Clay Dayman. She was surprised to see a tiny light lurking in the black depths of his eyes that clearly said 'Bravo' to her.

'You're sorry!' snarled an infuriated Doyle. 'Well, so am I! Sorry that Dayman's going to make that trip back without you. If, when you've had time to reconsider, you still want to go up North, then I'll make the arrangements. I'm surprised that you could even think of pulling up your roots and leaving us, let alone of leaving on the spur of the moment like that,' he added in an aggrieved tone that was supposed to reach through to Sheena's over-indulgent conscience.

Sheena recognised the tactics, but she was fighting for more than a tactical win. She was fighting for her future, for a future that held all she had ever wanted from life—marriage with Doyle, the man she loved.

Her lovely eyes held the challenge out to him as they met his. 'I have reconsidered, Doyle,' she answered firmly. 'And I've decided to accept Mr Dayman's escort. I'm sure your mother can find a replacement for me—there's a scarcity of jobs at the moment and there's bound to be a lot of applicants to choose from.' She gave a whimsical smile. 'It's not as if I had a future here, is it?' she asked him softly, 'and it's time I thought about my future.'

'My sentiments entirely,' said Clay Dayman dryly.

'You keep out of this!' Doyle thundered at him. 'What do you know about it anyway?'

'More than you think,' answered Clay with a hint of warning in his voice, and Sheena, although she didn't know this man very well, suspected that he was enjoying riling Doyle. 'I promised James Greig that I would look out for his daughter, and I guess that gives me the right to throw in my weight. I would have liked to have given Miss Greig a few more days' preparation before we leave, but I've a heavy schedule on back home and can't afford to take more than a couple of days off.' His dark penetrating eyes fixed on Doyle in what looked like a challenging manner to Sheena.

'Running the business singlehanded now, are you?' sneered Doyle. 'You've a smallholding too, have you?'

Sheena held her breath. She had never known Doyle speak to anyone like that before. If Clay Dayman was spoiling for a fight then so was Doyle.

Clay's eyebrows lifted, and Sheena noticed how expressive they were and how their winged blackness gave him a look of hauteur. 'Well, it's a holding,' he drawled non-committally, 'but I wouldn't call it all that small.'

His calm answer and refusal to rise to Doyle's taunt put him in a more advantageous position, and Doyle was quick to note this.

'I'd like to speak to Sheena alone,' he said in a

manner meant to prove to Clay that he was boss of that territory.

Clay inclined his head in agreement, but his narrowed eyes proved that he was not keen on this suggestion. He walked to the study door and turned to Sheena before he left. 'I'll be leaving early tomorrow. If you're coming, be packed and ready to leave by seven,' he told her, and with a curt nod in Doyle's direction, he left.

Sheena stared at the closed door, then back at Doyle also looking at the door with a grim expression on his face. 'You didn't even thank him for returning the money, Doyle,' she said sadly.

Doyle's lips clamped together. 'I might have done,' he replied grimly, 'if he hadn't had the nerve to think he could just walk in here and whisk you back to some outlying broken-down holding. And what you're thinking of in agreeing to go with him is beyond me. What do you know about the man? Nothing! What sort of a man would give a stranger a job without looking into his background?' His jaw squared. 'He must have been hard up for help, that's all I can say!'

'Or he might be a very kind man who wanted to help someone,' answered Sheena quietly. 'Father didn't use that money he stole, and he must have needed work of some kind,' she reminded him.

'Then more fool he,' Doyle rapped out scathingly. 'He took it, didn't he? He might just as well have used it.'

Sheena winced at this bald statement. All the hurt

and shame she had undergone for the past three years washed over her again. The fact that her father had not used the money and had returned it to Doyle, counted for nothing in Doyle's eyes.

His aggression vanished as he looked at Sheena and he put an arm around her slim waist. 'Think what it cost me, Sheena,' he said softly. 'We would have been married but for that.'

Sheena moved away from his encircling arm. He hadn't chosen a very good time to show her that he still cared. 'And now, Doyle?' she said, her clear eyes searching his.

Her heart was thudding as she waited for his reply. He looked away from her and stared at the saddle-bag now lying between them on the study floor. She felt the coldness gathering around them and knew that nothing had changed. She would go North— anything was better than this. Doyle would marry one of his mother's friends' daughters. Perhaps that was what he was waiting for? For her to leave the way clear for him.

She turned and made for the door and at his urgent, 'Wait, Sheena!' she faced him. 'It's all right, Doyle,' she said wearily. 'I ought to have known better. Will you tell your mother I'll be leaving in the morning?' She did not wait for a reply, but went straight to her room to start her packing.

CHAPTER TWO

SHEENA was packed long before lunch, wishing she could walk out then and there, and chiding herself for not having had the foresight to ask Clay Dayman where he was staying.

He had said that he had come fifty miles that morning, and that meant that he had probably come from Sydney, but it was unlikely that he had returned there, not if he was calling for her at seven the next morning.

She knew that there were many homesteads around that would oblige a traveller for an overnight stay, although the nearest would be about ten miles away. If he hadn't used quite such a blunt approach to Doyle, he would have spend the night at Barter's Ridge, she thought wretchedly. Although in all fairness, Doyle's attitude had been belligerent from the start, and had not exactly smoothed the way for good relations.

Her two medium-sized cases stood beside her bed, and held all that she possessed in the world. She and her father had moved into furnished quarters at the station, so there were no other encumbrances for her to worry about. Her main worry now was not to let herself get talked out of her decision.

Mrs Charter might put up a feeble resistance to the

move, for the sake of protocol if nothing else, but would inwardly welcome such an event. Sheena was certain that her thinking ran along the same lines as hers in that Doyle was biding his time in choosing her successor, and once she had gone, there would be a spate of suitable applicants paraded for his inspection.

Sheena closed her eyes to shut out these thoughts; at least she wouldn't be around to witness his mother's determined bid to find him a wife.

There was a light tap on her door, and Sheena squared her slim shoulders. It could be Doyle, or his mother. She glanced at her watch before she went to answer the knock. It was twelve-thirty. It would not be Doyle, she thought with an inward sigh of relief. Today was pay day for the station hands, and he would be away at the men's quarters for the pay-out and would then be off to the outlying settlements to settle their accounts, not returning until nightfall.

When she opened the door it was not Mrs Charter, but Cookie who stood there with a tray in her hand and an anxious look in her kindly brown eyes. 'Thought you might like some sustenance,' she said brightly, and carried the tray into the room, setting it down on the bedside table. It was then that she saw the cases and turned to Sheena. 'You going somewhere?' she queried lightly, but her look was a worried one as it rested on Sheena.

'To the North,' replied Sheena, 'tomorrow.'

'Tomorrow?' echoed Cookie. 'For how long?' she demanded. 'That Ranger—was it about your father?'

Sheena nodded. 'He's not a Ranger, Cookie. His name is Clay Dayman, and he owns some property in Bellingen. Dad worked for him,' she replied slowly.

'Your dad...?' Cookie began hesitantly.

'He's dead,' Sheena answered tonelessly. 'I don't know when it happened, or how. He left Mr Dayman a letter telling him where he'd hidden the money he took. Mr Dayman brought it back to Doyle.'

Cookie sank slowly on to the bed as she digested this news. 'You going for the funeral?' she asked.

Sheena shook her head. 'Mr Dayman didn't mention it. I guess that part of it was over with by the time he got the letter from Father.' She was silent for a moment or two, then added. 'I'm going for good, Cookie. Father left me a letter too. He had a small-holding of sorts and he's left it to me.' She looked hastily away from the sympathy she saw in Cookie's eyes. 'It's for the best, Cookie,' she added firmly. 'It's time I struck out on my own.'

'Doyle?' asked Cookie. 'Surely the return of the money...?'

Sheena shrugged expressively. 'Apparently not,' she replied, managing to inject a dry note into her voice, knowing full well what Cookie was referring to. 'Now that the money has been returned, I'm free to do as I wish.'

Cookie's plump hands spread out in a gesture of hopelessness. 'Pride, Sheena, that's all it is. The Charters have always had too much pride. Even so,' she said thoughtfully, 'Doyle won't like it, and don't tell me different. I'd swear he had a row with that man that was here. He looked like thunder when he left for the pay-out.'

'I don't think Mr Dayman was in a good mood, either,' commented Sheena with a wry smile. 'They didn't exactly hit it off from the beginning.'

Cookie gave a start at this and fumbled in her apron pocket. 'I forgot to give you this,' she said, and handed Sheena a scrap of paper obviously torn out of a recipe book. It had an address on it. 'He gave me that as he left,' she said, 'and I had to jot it down before I forgot it. It's where he's staying tonight.'

Sheena looked at the address. 'Marshall's Way' was the name of the property, and she frowned. 'Where's that, Cookie?' she asked perplexedly.

Cookie lifted her plump shoulders. 'I thought I knew every homestead from here to Sydney,' she replied, 'but that's a new one on me. That's why I wrote it down.'

It was not much use having the address if she did not know where the property was, Sheena thought with an inward sigh.

Cookie suddenly sat up straight. 'It's old Mr Bounty's place! It must be!' she exclaimed. 'Remember it was bought by a lawyer from Windsor a few months ago?' she reminded Sheena, with a note of satisfaction in her voice for having unravelled the mystery.

Sheena's frown lifted. 'You're right, Cookie. It must be!' she replied, feeling a surge of relief flow over her, for the property was only fifteen miles away fom Barter's Ridge, and hardly any distance by car.

The news uplifted her, and she no longer felt alone.

She had been dreading the last evening spent at Barter's Ridge. Usually she had dinner with the family, but if they had company Sheena deliberately absented herself, and ate with Cookie in the kitchen. She was thinking of the miserable meal ahead of her that evening, with a furious Doyle bent on making her change her mind and Mrs Carter having to add her weight to the argument, in spite of her personal thoughts on the matter. 'If only I could go now,' she said, speaking her thoughts aloud.

Cookie gave her a hurt look that made her feel immediately contrite. 'Oh, I didn't really mean it like that, Cookie,' she added hastily. 'I shall miss you all terribly, but I have to go, you do see that, don't you? I might not get another chance.'

A slow nod of the head showed that Cookie agreed with Sheena on this point. 'Some folk don't know when they're well off,' she commented sadly. 'No one holds anything against you.' She gave an expressive shrug and sighed loudly. 'Of course, if you did marry Doyle, then the pussies would get to work, there's no doubt of that. Sheer blind frustration on the part of the disappointed mammas would ensure that, but you've the disposition to ride all that if the Charters could only swallow their pride—as it is——' She got up from the bed and patted Sheena on the shoulder in a motherly way. 'You go, girl. You're better out of it.'

Sheena gave her a slight hug. 'I knew you'd understand, Cookie,' she said mistily.

Cookie turned away swiftly so that Sheena would

not see the mistiness gathering in her own eyes. 'Well, I suppose I ought to get on. The Maxtons are coming to dinner, and you know how fussed the Missus gets if things aren't served on time, and she's chosen a fancy menu to outdo Mrs. Maxton's last dinner party.'

Sheena's eyes lit up. 'I didn't know there was going to be company this evening,' she exclaimed, as she felt a rush of relief flow over her at the thought that her presence would not be required at the dinner table.

'I was only told this morning,' grumbled Cookie. 'I suppose the Maxtons' French cook is having one of her temperamental lapses again. It wouldn't be so bad if those two didn't try to compete against each other like they do. It's like being in the middle of a firing line,' she added dolefully as she left.

As Sheena ate a little of the light lunch Cookie had brought her, she wondered if Cookie's surmise about the Maxtons' cook throwing a tantrum was true. She had not known about the dinner party before the morning break or she would have told Sheena. It had been shortly after their coffee break that Clay Dayman had arrived, so the dinner party had been arranged since then.

Sheena could not be certain, but she could see the advantage such an arrangement would bring to what must be a very anxious Mrs Charter. She would be terrified that Doyle would ask Sheena to marry him rather than lose her, and this was the last thing Mrs Charter wanted to happen.

Her choice of guests for this very sudden dinner

party, added to Sheena's calculations that it was a deliberate ploy to distract Doyle from such a disastrous course. The Maxtons had a very pretty daughter who had had the right upbringing to satisfy Amelia Charter's strict sense of social pride, and there was no denying that Doyle liked Jenny Maxton, and Jenny adored Doyle.

Sheena pushed away her half-finished plate of salad on this thought. She liked Jenny Maxton, and although the thought hurt, she would rather Doyle married her than one of the two other contenders that Mrs Charter had in mind.

Her heart went out to Doyle who would now be sitting at the large old office table in the manager's office, personally attending to the pay-out. He had always carried out this task, although the manager was quite capable of looking after this side of affairs for him.

Sheena had often sat beside him during their courting days, listening to his authoritative voice answering whatever queries the men had, and giving them an opportunity to air their grievances since most of them worked in the outlying sections of the station. Thus it was a payout and a general chat occasion that could not be hurried, and saved Doyle the necessity of having to rush off to distant sections in order to settle any disputes that arose during the working day.

She remembered the way he would suddenly look at her with a message in his eyes saying that he loved her, and her heart would pound in anticipation of the time when they would be alone together and he would kiss her into the land of paradise.

Sheena's small hands clenched together. His love had not been strong enough to withstand her father's folly in taking that money. She no longer thought of it as a crime. He hadn't spent the money, and she couldn't understand why he had succumbed to temptation in the first place. He was getting a good wage—all Doyle's men were well paid. They had no debts, and although not rich, they had all that they needed. At least, she had thought so, but apparently her father must have wanted other things. She had been so caught up in the whirl of Doyle's courtship that she had not noticed anything different about him. He had always been a quiet man, and she knew that the loss of her mother had hit him hard, although he had never said so.

She swallowed. Thinking about these things did not make her situation any easier. It was done with, as were her hopes of a future as Doyle's wife.

As if to thrust these memories away from her, Sheena got up hastily and picked up the tray to take down to the kitchen. She would have to see Mrs Charter, and now was as good a time as any. Doyle would have told her the news, of this she was certain, since she could not have been ignorant of the fact that Sheena had had a visitor that morning, and would have made a point of quizzing Doyle on the matter. There was not a great deal that Mrs Charter missed on the home front.

Cookie was busy making vol-au-vent cases when she entered the kitchen, and Sheena promised to give

her a hand after she had had a word with Mrs
Charter. 'I'd better get it over with,' she commented
with an ironic smile.

'You'll have to wait until this evening, then,' replied Cookie, putting a thin coating of flour on her
pastry board. 'She's out visiting the Frosts, and that
means that she won't be back until sevenish.'

Sheena's gaze fixed on the pastry board. This appeared to be a day of unexpected happenings. Mrs
Charter had said nothing of a visit to the Frost family
the day before. They were their nearest neighbours
on the southern boundary, and far enough away to
ensure an afternoon's absence for the visitor. It
could have been a coincidence that she had chosen
that afternoon for the visit, Sheena thought, but she
very much doubted it, and instinctively knew that she
was not going to be given a chance of a private word
with her before she left the following morning.

As she took an apron out of the dresser drawer
and put it on, her feelings were mixed. She was relieved that she had been saved the necessity of listening to Mrs Charter's insincere lamentations on losing
her so suddenly. On the other hand, it seemed a poor
return for her past service to the family, and she had
done nothing to deserve this parting snub on Amelia
Charter's part.

It just went to show, she thought with an inward
sigh, that she had never forgiven Sheena for her
audacity in setting her sights on her son. It would
never occur to her that Doyle was old enough to
make his own decisions, particularly when it came

to choosing his bride, and at thirty-one, well past any guidance on that score from his mother. On any other matter, Doyle ruled the household as well as the station, and she would never dream of countermanding any order of his. If the decision had been hers, Sheena would never have been offered a post in the homestead. As it was, she had accepted his ruling on this, and had been careful to keep on the right side of Doyle by adopting a welcoming attitude towards her.

Given the time, Sheena was sure she would have engineered Doyle's absence from Barter's Ridge until after her departure, and had not been slow off the mark in arranging some distraction in the form of a dinner party that ensured his presence until late that evening.

Doyle would see beyond the tactic, of course, Sheena was sure, and whether it was successful was entirely up to him, she thought as she started to mix a sauce for the vol-au-vents. Her soft lips firmed as she recalled the way his eyes had not met hers when she had challenged him in the study. She caught her breath as a ragged sob threatened to escape. She loved him, but he didn't love her. He wanted her, and must have put an iron restraint on his physical yearnings where she was concerned.

All these things she could now see clearly. She ought to have left a long time ago, but she had been so sure that one day things would come right for them, and it was about time that she faced up to the truth, no matter how much it hurt.

Sheena stayed helping Cookie for the rest of the afternoon, and left her to it when all the preparations were finished. 'I'll miss you, Sheena,' said Cookie wistfully, as Sheena took her apron off and placed it back in the dresser drawer for the last time.

'I'll miss you too, Cookie,' replied Sheena in a low tone. 'I'll see you later. I shall have to do a swift round of goodbyes this evening down at the men's quarters. I couldn't very well go without saying anything, could I?' she commented sadly, then smiled at Cookie. 'I'm glad it's going to be only you and me for dinner. It's just what I would have wanted,' she added softly, as she left the kitchen.

Sheena's goodbyes took a little longer than she had anticipated. Part of her youth had been spent with the station hands, and although she had not seen much of them since she had been installed at the homestead, little messages of cheer had been sent through to her via Cookie's brother Len, who was in charge of the station stores and who made a point of visiting the homestead kitchen on baking days.

These messages had cheered Sheena as they were meant to do. Sent by the tough, often uncommunicative men who worked in all weathers, the messages were simple and sincere and all the more heartening because of this, as were their good wishes for her future. As Sheena made her way back to the homestead, her thoughts remained on the men she had just said farewell to. There had been no searching questions asked, only a sort of tacit approval for what she was doing. As if, she mused, as she reached the homestead, they were fully aware of her situation and wholeheartedly agreed with her decision to cut loose. They knew of course that her engagement to Doyle had been broken, news travels fast on a station, particularly that sort of news, and it did occur to her that perhaps they thought Doyle was to blame. In a way he was, yet it had been Sheena who had handed the ring back and he had accepted it.

She was about to pass the study window on her way to the back quarters of the homestead when Doyle's voice arrested her in her tracks. 'She won't go, I tell you!' The words were uttered in a harsh tone. 'She knows where she's well off. Can you imagine her coping with a tatty rundown smallholding?'

Sheena did not wait to hear any more, but hastily retraced her steps and went the long way round the homestead towards the kitchen quarters.

A glance at her watch told her that it was seven-thirty, and dinner was at eight, not leaving him much time to change in time to meet his guests who ought to be arriving any time now. It looked as if his mother had left nothing to chance by seeking him out as soon as he arrived back from the pay-out, anxious to ascertain that Doyle would not stand in Sheena's way.

But he did intend to stand in her way, Sheena thought wretchedly as she entered the kitchen now filled with appetising smells, but with no sign of Cookie, who Sheena surmised was now changing into what she always alluded to as her 'serving-up dress', ready to wait on table during dinner. He had

sounded so sure of himself too, she thought, as she
went through the kitchen and made her way to her
bedroom, thankful that the room that she had been
allotted was in an added wing of the original struc-
ture of the homestead, and built to accommodate the
staff. Cookie's room was the next door but one, down
the passage, and they shared the bathroom facilities.

With such an arrangement, Sheena was able to
keep out of Doyle's way in her off-duty hours, and
she had often been thankful for this thoughtful if
preserving action on Mrs Charter's part in choosing
her accommodation.

Closing her bedroom door behind her, Sheena
looked at her cases. She *was* going! Did Doyle really
think she was so spineless? And that all he had to do
was to talk her out of it? If he did, then he had a surprise coming! She had taken a lot during the last
three years and she was done with subservience. The
money had been returned and she had no need to feel
constantly guilty about her father's folly.

She would stay only if Doyle asked her to marry
him. Her soft lips twisted at the thought; she wasn't
going to give up now. As Clay Dayman had put it,
she had played her part.

For some reason that she couldn't define, the
thought of the tall dark stranger gave her the courage
that she might have lacked earlier. It was not only the
fact that he had returned the money—it went deeper
than that. There was something utterly reassuring
about the man, and Sheena instinctively felt that she
could put her complete faith in him. This was

strange, for his features were hard and forbidding and she had sensed that he was not a man to suffer fools gladly. Yet he had come all this way to fulfil an obligation to her father, who had only been an employee of his.

When she thought of the way that he had forced her hand in the study and made her stand up to Doyle, she shook her head bewilderedly. She had wanted to contradict him, but found herself completely unable to do so, and when she recalled the look in his eyes after she had accepted the challenge that he had thrown out to her, she knew an extraordinary sense of pride that she had pleased him.

At nine Sheena went down to the kitchen to have dinner with Cookie. By that time dinner would have been served and the coffee taken in.

'Jenny looks well,' Cookie commented casually, as she took two plates out of the hot plate rack and started to dish up their meal. 'Got a lovely dress on,' she added pensively. 'Looks as if she was all dressed up to go out somewhere and got roped in to joining her parents here.'

Sheena gave a casual nod as she stopped Cookie from putting too much on her plate. It all added up, she thought bitterly. Mrs Charter, it seemed, had lost no time in passing on the news of Sheena Greig's imminent departure from the scene. After her talk with Doyle a short time before the arrival of the Maxtons, she must now be a very frustrated woman, since from what Sheena had overheard, Doyle had no intention of letting her leave.

If she did but know it, she had no cause to worry. As the hours had ticked away since Clay Dayman's departure, so had Sheena's resolve strengthened. It was a now or never effort for her, there would be no second chance to make a bid for freedom from her emotional ties with Doyle.

All through dinner, Sheena had half expected Doyle to make an appearance and ask her to have a word with him in the study where they could be assured of privacy. When they had finished dinner and there had been no sign of any such appearance or request from him, Sheena's strong resolve almost vanished, and she felt wretchedly miserable.

This was Doyle's way of punishing her for even thinking of leaving. He wasn't going to speak to her, let alone plead with her to stay. She had felt low before, but never as low as she was at that time. His very absence was accusing. He had given her a home when she had nowhere to go, and this was the way that she had repaid him. But she had worked for her board, a small voice argued inside her, she had taken nothing for granted.

As miserable as she was, Sheena had the sense to see that it was better this way. Had Doyle made a determined bid to keep her, she wasn't all that sure of her ability to stand by her decision. There would be no Clay Dayman present at that meeting, and no one else to strengthen her cause.

It was just after ten-thirty that Sheena decided to turn in for the night. Tomorrow would be a long day, most of it spent travelling, and she was anxious for the morning to come. She wanted to get the leave-taking over with in the shortest possible time. Doyle was usually off early in the mornings and had left the homestead by six-thirty, but whether he would do so the following day was debatable.

After saying goodnight to Cookie, Sheena made her way to her quarters. The sound of laughter coming from the front porch of the homestead arrested her for a second as she passed on her way. She could imagine the scene. Doyle would be sitting in one of the cane chairs, probably next to Jenny. His mother, and Jenny's parents, would be seated nearby in the wisteria-scented porch. The tray of drinks would be on the table. That was part of Doyle's life that she had been excluded from for three years.

The echo of their laughter rebounded around her as she escaped to her room. That Doyle had been laughing too, hurt her far more than his non-appearance in the kitchen earlier.

Perhaps they were celebrating her departure, she thought distractedly, in which case she had better not disappoint them, she told herself, as she went through to the bathroom and took a quick shower.

She must remember to collect her toilet requisites the following morning, she thought as she towelled herself down and then liberally used the scented talcum powder that she and Cookie shared between them. She must leave that for Cookie, she thought, and pick some up for herself somewhere on the journey north.

It was this mundane kind of thinking that pre-

vented her from going to pieces. She was leaving and
Doyle was laughing; at all costs she had not to concentrate on that. He didn't love her at all, and if it
hadn't been for the timely intervention of a stranger,
she would have gone on pining her life away wrapped
in dreams that would never come true.

When she had finished in the bathroom she slipped
back to her bedroom draped in the large towel.

On closing her bedroom door she found herself
jerked round and held hard against the door, and her
quick gasp of astonishment was cut off by Doyle's
searching lips on hers. The smell of whisky was
strong on his breath, and as he was not normally a
heavy drinker, Sheena knew that he had overstepped
his quota.

When at last she was given respite, she attempted
to push him away from her, but she was only able to
use one hand, the other was grasping the towel in a
frantic effort to keep herself covered. 'For goodness'
sake, Doyle!' she gasped, 'wait outside until I'm
dressed. I'll talk to you then,' she urged frantically.

Doyle's reply was a firm shake of the head. 'After
we've got a few things straightened out,' he said
harshly, his voice slightly slurred. 'Firstly, you're not
going north with Dayman, got that?' His tone
changed to a cajoling one. 'Look, sweetheart, I know
it's been tough for you. It's been tough for me, too,
having you so near yet so far from me. I ought to
have sent you away, but I couldn't, and I'm damned
if I'll let you walk out with a stranger. I've always
watched over you, haven't I?'

He shook his head as if to try and clear his thoughts. 'Look,' he said abruptly, 'a friend of mine's got an apartment in Sydney, and he's putting it up for rent. We'll take it. You'll go tomorrow morning as you've planned, but not to the North. I'm taking you to Sydney.'

Sheena's eyes widened as the implication of what he was saying sunk through to her bewildered senses, and she shook her head.

'It's going to work out, honey,' he urged her softly. 'I'll spend every weekend with you. You didn't think I'd let you go, did you?'

'I'm going!' Sheena got out breathlessly, but her voice trembled. 'You can't stop me, Doyle. You don't love me,' she said, as she shook her arm free from his restraining hold. 'I'd prefer to forget what you've just suggested. The answer's no all along the line!' she got out on a raw sob.

Doyle caught her arm again and she winced as his strong fingers bit into her soft flesh. 'I can and will stop you making the greatest mistake of your life,' he said harshly. 'What difference does a ceremony make, anyway? You were meant to be mine, so stop fooling yourself.'

Sheena wanted to scream at him that she had other values, and that if he really loved her, he wouldn't have insulted her like that. Yet when she replied her voice was low and bitter. 'Go back to your guests, Doyle, they'll be wondering where you've got to.'

Doyle's lips straightened, and he made a lunge towards her. 'I see you need some convincing,' he said harshly, and pulled her, struggling, into his arms.

'Doyle? Where are you?' Mrs Charter's querulous voice reached up to the determined Doyle, and the equally determined Sheena attempting to fend him off. 'Jenny's just off.'

Sheena saw Doyle's head go up in a gesture of frustrated fury. 'I'll be back,' he said grimly. 'One way or the other we're going to settle this tonight.'

As soon as the door had closed behind him, Sheena threw off the towel and with trembling fingers dressed in record time. She then snatched up her cases and running as fast as the weight of the cases allowed her, she reached Cookie's room.

Cookie was just in the act of fastening a sleeping net over her newly permanent waved hair when Sheena burst in on her. Hastily closing the door behind her, Sheena leaned back weakly against it. 'I've got to get out of here, Cookie,' she gasped out breathlessly. 'Please help me. Could Len run me over to Marshall's Way?' she asked, her lovely sapphire-blue eyes wide and pleading.

Cookie studied the trembling girl and noticed the way she hadn't bothered about her appearance. Her sweater was on back to front for a start, and she drew her own conclusions. She had seen the way Doyle's eyes had followed Sheena when she went about her duties, but had been careful to look the other way when Sheena was looking his way.

'There isn't much time,' Sheena urged on a note of panic.

'Time enough,' answered Cookie grimly, as she

took the hairnet off, and calmly collected her coat from the wardrobe and slipped it over her nightgown. Then she picked up one of Sheena's cases. 'We'll go out the side door,' she said, and then as a thought struck her she turned to Sheena. 'You wait here until I've seen if the coast is clear.'

A second later, she ushered Sheena out into the passage and towards the side door. There was the sound of an engine turning over and then spluttering to a stop. 'The Maxtons' car's playing up again,' she whispered to Sheena, as they slipped through the doorway and out into the backyard of the homestead. 'That'll keep them busy. The last time it happened it took the best part of thirty minutes to fix—I know, because it kept me awake.'

Once outside the homestead Sheena began to relax. As long as she could hear the constant revving and spluttering stops of the Maxtons' car as the men worked on the engine, she knew where Doyle was, and fervently hoped that it would take another thirty minutes to fix it this time. Cookie had gone to collect her brother Len whose quarters were above the stores, and if her luck continued to hold she should soon be on her way to Clay Dayman and safety.

When she heard the constant purring of an engine, her heartbeats increased rapidly. They had got the engine going! Oh, where were Cookie and Len? She strained her eyes against the blackness of the night trying to look ahead to see if she could see any sign of them—the stores were only a few minutes' walk from the back of the homestead.

Sheena was trying to calm herself by telling herself that even if Doyle and Mr Maxton had fixed the car, Doyle would have to have a clean-up before he went to find her, and that would give her another five minutes leeway. If only—her frantic calculations ended in a sigh of pure relief as the dark shape of a car loomed up beside her. It had been Len's car that she had heard, not the Maxtons' and as if to prove this to her, another prolonged burst of engine revving broke out behind her, coming from the front of the house.

'He doesn't know where Mr Dayman is, does he, Cookie?' Sheena asked breathlessly, as she got into the car after Len had placed her cases in the boot.

There was no need for names to be mentioned. 'No, and he's not going to,' replied Cookie soothingly. 'Len knows when to hold his tongue.'

'I'll let you have my address as soon as I'm settled,' Sheena whispered, as Cookie closed the car door behind her. 'And thanks, Cookie, for everything,' she added on a thankful sounding note as the car started off.

'Lend a hand here, will you?' Sheena heard Doyle call out, as they swept out of the yard and on to the main driveway, but Len kept going and Sheena was thankful that Doyle would not know whose car it was that had just left the premises, as there were two entrances to the homestead and they were taking the rear entrance. No doubt when he discovered that Sheena had gone he would make some enquiries, but all the permanent staff at Barter's Ridge possessed transport of one kind or another, and though he might suspect that Len had had a hand in Sheena's flight from the homestead, he couldn't prove it.

There was his pride to take into consideration too, thought Sheena unhappily. Although he might be genuinely worried about her, he would not be able to make a big thing about her departure, as a fuss would raise a few unwanted questions as to the reason why she had taken off so suddenly. No, she thought sadly: Doyle would not make a move to find her until the next day. Under the circumstances, he couldn't.

CHAPTER THREE

SHEENA did not know the property now named 'Marshall's Way', but Len did, and as they drove through the boundary gates and on to the homestead precinct he made several comments on alterations that had been carried out since he had last visited. 'Looks as if it's going to be a grand place now that some money's being spent on it,' he said in a cogitative way that required no comment from Sheena, and this was just as well as she was busy wondering just what she could say to whoever answered the door when they arrived at the homestead.

By the time they drew up in front of a large redbrick bungalow with a wide verandah running the length of the residence, Sheena's imagination had got her confronted by an indignant-looking owner of the property who had told her in no uncertain terms that this was no decent time for a young lady to pay a visit on his guest, and to be gone about her business.

Her trepidation heightened when she saw that apart from a low lighted lamp on the porch, there were no other lights on in the bungalow. To be confronted by an indignant owner was one thing, but when that same person had had to be dragged out of bed on such a summons—the thought made Sheena's knees go weak as she walked up the steps to the porch.

The comforting presence of Len, however, who had taken her cases out of the trunk and now stood beside her as she rang the bell, gave her the courage to see it through.

It could not have been much longer than a few seconds before her ring was answered, but to the apprehensive Sheena it seemed minutes during which she rehearsed her opening speech, but had not got much further than asking to speak to Mr Dayman.

As she saw the tall, and at that moment, extremely comforting form of the very man that she had wanted to see, Sheena's vast relief stemmed her rehearsed explanation, and all she could manage was a weak smile at him.

Without seeking any such explanation, Clay Dayman stood aside in a silent gesture that told her to go inside and collected the cases from Len with a mild, 'Good! Now we can get an early start tomorrow.'

As Sheena thanked Len for his help, and at his stern request that she write and let them know how she fared, to which she gave her promise, she found time to wonder at Clay Dayman's acceptance of her arrival at that time of night. Almost, she mused, as if he had been expecting such an event. But of course, he couldn't have done, and once again she found herself thinking that he was an exceptionally extraordinary man, to whom she had good cause to be grateful.

Len too, it seemed, had formed his own opinion,

and had come down heavily on the credit side of the man he had brought Sheena to. She had not missed the quiet summing up he had given Clay Dayman during those first few minutes, and knew that in spite of his sister's assurance on the credibility of the stranger, he would not have left her there but taken her elsewhere should he have had any doubts on the matter.

When Len had left, Sheena stood inside the hall of the bungalow and watched Clay close the door and latch it. Reaction was now setting in, and she felt mentally and physically exhausted. 'I must apologise for not letting you know I was coming this evening,' she began hesitatingly, not quite knowing how to explain her sudden arrival.

Clay gave her a swift searching look before he picked up her cases. 'You look all in to me,' he commented firmly. 'I suggest you turn in. You can use the guest room at the end of the passage,' he went on, as he walked ahead of her and indicated that she should follow him. 'The bed's made up. I was going to use it, but I can switch to the main bedroom, John's away on a case right now.'

Sheena's tired brain simply refused to function properly as she followed Clay's tall straight back down the passage. 'John?' she murmured in a puzzled way.

Clay put her cases down and pushed open the door of a room at the end of the passage. 'My brother,' he said, 'he owns the place.'

Sheena watched him put the cases down by a made

up single bed and thought confusedly that she ought to at least offer to help make up the bed that he would be using, seeing that she was taking his. 'Can I help you with yours?' she queried, attempting to shake off the tiredness that had suddenly enveloped her. 'It's much easier with two, isn't it?' she added. 'I mean, one can stand one side, and one the other,' she tacked on lamely, determinedly blinking her eyes to keep them open.

'You'd better get to bed before you fall flat on your face,' said Clay firmly but with a trace of amusement in his voice. 'I can manage, thank you,' and at Sheena's lame attempt at protest he added softly, 'And no arguing. We've a long journey ahead of us tomorrow.' With that he left her and closed the door firmly behind him.

The rest of that night was a complete blur to Sheena, who didn't remember getting undressed and into the bed, although all she did was to remove her skirt and sweater and shoes and thankfully slip in between the cool sheets and into oblivion.

When she awoke the following morning she wondered what had awakened her, for when she opened her eyes it was barely light, then she heard a sharp tap on her door. 'Breakfast in ten minutes. The bathroom's all yours.'

This last statement brought Sheena out of her lethargy and she sat up sharply and gazed around her. Through the pale dawn light she could make out the unfamiliar shapes of the furniture of the room she was in, and as she did so recollection of the pre-

vious evening's happening flooded over her, leaving
her feeling lost and utterly miserable.

This time yesterday morning she would be just
awakening and listening to the activity in the yards
at the back of the homestead as she had done every
morning since she had moved into the homestead.
She would strain to hear Doyle's voice as he gave in-
structions to the waiting men before he left on his
tour of inspection of the outer pastures. She swallowed hard. It was no use remembering things like
that now, she told herself as she scrambled hastily out
of bed and searched in her case for her toilet bag.

She located the bathroom that was next to her bedroom and took a hasty shower, then back in the bedroom she searched out something more suitable to
wear for the journey north.

The activity kept her busy, but her thoughts kept
returning to Barter's Ridge, and inevitably to Doyle
and what he intended to do about her abrupt removal
from the homestead.

As she left her room and went in search of the kitchen—not a difficult task as the appetising smell of
eggs and bacon sizzling led her in the right direction
—she wondered if she ought to ring through and
leave a message for Doyle to the effect that she had
joined Mr Dayman and would be travelling north
with him.

If she could only be sure that Doyle had left the
homestead on his rounds, this would be the correct
thing to do, but if he hadn't—and if he just happened
to answer the phone—Sheena hastily discarded any

further thoughts on this matter. She would ring up Barter's Ridge once they had got to their destination and she would ring the manager's number so that he could pass the message on to Doyle. That way she could avoid speaking direct to him and not find herself being harassed into giving him her address.

When she entered the kitchen the tall form of Clay Dayman was standing by the gleaming oven and dishing up their breakfast. 'Two eggs or one?' he asked in his deep finely moulded voice.

Sheena knew an instant feeling of acute embarrassment. She didn't really know this man, yet here she was taking breakfast with him before starting out on a new chapter of her life—a chapter in which, she suspected, he would have more that a passing interest.

Her clear direct gaze met his dark inscrutable one as she answered, 'Only one, please. I don't usually have a cooked breakfast.'

He turned his attention back to the pan he was holding, and placed one egg on a plate warming on the hot rack above the oven, then added one rasher of bacon and handed the plate to her. 'That enough?' he queried with a lifted eyebrow.

Sheena nodded, took the plate from him and walked over to the table where knives and forks had been laid ready for use.

Clay brought his loaded plate to the table too and motioned that Sheena should tuck in. 'I hope you're not going to discover an enormous appetite in the middle of the morning,' he commented, as he began his breakfast and stared direct at Sheena. 'I intend making one stop at Newcastle, and one stop only. Okay? With any luck we should arrive mid-afternoon. You're a good traveller, I hope?'

Sheena blinked. 'I think so,' she managed to get out, wondering just what she had landed herself with. There were shades of Doyle in his autocratic orders, making her feel compelled to comply no matter what her own thoughts on the matter were.

Her eyes remained on Clay Dayman as he ate his meal, and she knew an irrational rush of panic and tried to calm herself by making an assessment of him. His white short-sleeved silk shirt, that was open at the neck to give the maximum coolness for the heat of the day to come, showed a mass of dark thickly curled hair just visible against the whiteness of the shirt, and gave an impression of physical strength, as did his long well-tanned bare arms. His grey corded pants that fitted snug to his long waistline had obviously been made to measure and were of the finest quality. Sheena didn't know much about men's clothes and could only go by Doyle's wardrobe, but Doyle was an immaculate dresser. Only the best was good enough for him, and he could afford to indulge himself.

Her gaze returned to Clay Dayman's face. A strong jaw, she mused, that showed a certain amount of determination. A man not easily beaten. His dark features reminded her of the stories that she had read as a child about gypsies. Of handsome, bold men who had their own mysterious customs and ways, who, because of their closeness with nature, knew more than the ordinary mortal, and used these powers to gain their objectives in life. A slight shiver ran through her as she recalled the way he had accepted her arrival the previous evening. Had he known she was coming?

What if she told him that she had changed her mind? she wondered. She hadn't liked the way he had laid down their travelling arrangements, making her feel an unwanted passenger. It was he who had sought her out, not she who had asked if she could accompany him back to the North.

At this point Clay looked up suddenly at her, and she saw a questioning look in his dark eyes before she hastily bent over her plate and made an attempt to raise an appetite that had temporarily deserted her.

'Want to make a last call at Barter's Ridge?' he shot out at her, as he pushed his empty plate away and reached for the coffee pot, pouring out two cups, leaving his black and pushing the cream jug towards her for her use.

Sheena quickly shook her head as she envisaged meeting a furious Doyle.

Clay's eyes remained fixed speculatively on her as he said softly, 'A pity. I was looking forward to re-arranging Charter's good looks.'

Sheena, taking a sip of her coffee, choked on this last statement and stared at him. Then a dull flush spread over her features. He couldn't know, she told herself, he was only guessing. To spare herself the embarrassment of having to think up a lie for her abrupt arrival the previous evening, she said quickly, 'If you mean to have a row with Doyle, then it's entirely unnecessary.' Then she added primly, 'I think fighting is undignified.' He could make what he liked of that, she thought.

'More undignified than having to hare out of your employer's place in the dead of the night, with just enough on to appear respectable?' Clay queried with a glint in his eyes.

Sheena gasped. 'I was dressed!' she replied indignantly, too surprised to wonder at his observant eyes.

'Oh, sure,' he answered, giving her an assessing look. 'Sweater on back to front, skirt unzipped, and precious little on underneath unless I'm mistaken,' he added grimly.

Sheena put her coffee cup down with a hand that shook. Even if he had noticed these things, it was hardly gentlemanly of him to mention them, she thought bleakly, let alone make trouble for Doyle by bringing it into the open. Her large sapphire blue eyes stared at Clay. She was beginning to have serious doubts about his integrity.

'Just in case you get any wrong ideas,' he remarked dryly, 'I was brought up with three sisters. John and I were what you might call outnumbered,' he added, still in that cool conversational manner, and Sheena sensed he was trying to put her at her ease and that meant that he had rightly gauged her thoughts on the matter.

She swallowed and shook her head. 'I don't want any trouble,' she said quietly, and quickly looked away from his searching eyes. 'You don't understand,' she added in a low voice.

'Don't I?' Clay answered swiftly, now back to the grim tone. 'Now you listen to me, Sheena. It's my guess that you had a narrow escape back there. I don't know how you happened to foil Charter's attempt to keep you chained to his side, and I'm putting it nicely. There's another word for what nearly happened, and you're not so innocent that you don't know what I'm talking about. I'll spare your blushes so far, but I'm warning you not to dress it up in a rosy light. As it happened, luck was on your side, but it might not have been, just remember that in future. If you want to go on loving a clay idol, then that's up to you. I guess there are some women that go for that kind of heel.'

Sheena's head jerked up at this and she gave Clay a warning look out of the blue fire that now shone in her eyes. He nodded grimly. 'I said heel,' he repeated slowly. 'And you might as well face it. If he thought anything about you in that way, then he'd have sent you away or he would have married you. He did neither.' With that he finished his coffee and got up. 'Time we were moving,' he said abruptly.

Sheena's coffee cup was still half full, but she did not attempt to finish it, feeling it would choke her. She had no defence to offer in his condemnation of Doyle, and that hurt. It was so easy for other people to judge, she thought bitterly, but what would Clay Dayman have done in the same circumstances?

While she collected the used crockery a tiny voice

inside her whispered that nothing would turn such a
man as he off his intended course. If Doyle had been
Clay Dayman, then he would have married her, of
that she had no doubt whatsoever, and it made her
feel doubly wretched.

Within ten minutes they were on the road travelling north. Sheena in a cotton blouse and jeans, sitting beside Clay and trying not to think about Doyle
and what might have been, and desperately trying
to look forward to a new life.

As they passed the familiar landscape that Sheena
knew so well and headed north, she felt as if part of
her was being wrenched away from her and it was
painful. She had no bright tomorrow and simply
nothing to look forward to. She was going to
live among strangers, and recalling Doyle's scathing
comments about her incapability of running a rundown smallholding, she almost burst into tears.

Only the thought of what would have happened
if she had stayed kept her from breaking down. She
still had her pride if nothing else. Her dreams lay in
tatters, but she would preserve them, no matter what
Clay Dayman thought. There would be no one else
for her, she was Doyle's, and would always be.

Soon they were in the midst of a long stream of
traffic and her eye caught the sight of a young couple
canoodling in the back of the car in front of them,
then she turned her look elsewhere with an abrupt
movement that caused Clay to give her a quick
glance before turning his attention to the road again.

Why had she to see something like that? she asked

herself miserably. Wasn't she unhappy enough, without being reminded that some people were lucky and had their dreams realised?

The tears that she had held at bay for so long, now cascaded down her cheeks, and though she despised herself for her weakness she was unable to do anything about it, and kept her head turned away from Clay so that he would not know that she was crying.

Once they came, it seemed they would never stop, and Sheena was powerless against the great flood of emotion that had been let loose within her. She could see nothing of the road, everything was blurred by the torrent of tears and the need to release the tension inside her.

'Here,' said Clay abruptly, shoving a box of tissues in her lap.

After giving him a surprised look, Sheena started pulling out several tissues. 'I'm very sorry,' she gulped. 'It's very stupid of me, but I really——' Down came another flood of tears stemming her watery apologies, and she buried her face in the tissues as if they could somehow stop the flow.

'Well, at least you don't blub,' murmured Clay. 'That I couldn't put up with. I guess it's as well for you to get it out of your system. Go ahead. You'll feel much better for it. I've a feeling you should have done that a long time ago,' he added ruminatively.

This quiet comment provided Sheena with the spur she so badly needed to put a brake on her emotions. He was having another dig at Doyle, she thought. Anyone would think Doyle had beaten her twice a day! Instead of which he had found a home for her and had found a job for her, and she loved him desperately. At this thought the brake slipped, and she was groping for another tissue to mop up with again.

Eventually the tears stopped flowing, leaving her calmer but utterly drained. The heat of the morning was now penetrating into the car and she leaned her head against the window. Within a space of seconds she had fallen asleep.

When she awoke she was aware of an ache in her neck and she gingerly rubbed the area while getting her bearings. They were still on the road and travelling at a steady cruising rate. The scenery that met her sleep-misted eyes was totally unfamiliar to her, for they were passing along a coastal road.

'So you've come to, have you?' commented Clay Dayman as he negotiated a bend in the road, handling the large powerful car with practised ease. 'We've just passed Macksville, and have about thirty miles to do.' He gave the still drowsy Sheena a quick questioning stare before he looked ahead again. 'I can stop at one of the roadside restaurants if you'd like a break. You were still out for the count at Newcastle,' he added dryly.

Sheena blinked at this news. She had been asleep for the better part of the long journey. Thirty miles, she reasoned, was hardly any distance, and she was sure that Clay Dayman was anxious to keep going. 'As we're so near we might as well keep going,' she answered, only just managing to stifle a yawn.

She knew her answer had pleased him by his curt nod of the head and his, 'We'll get a late lunch when we arrive. We're well ahead of time.

As the miles slid by, Sheena's thoughts turned to the life ahead of her. She was now fully awake and slightly apprehensive as to what lay in her future. 'What kind of a smallholding did my father have?' she asked Clay.

Without turning his attention from the road Clay replied, 'Fodder crops. A few pigs, and vegetables.'

Sheena stared ahead of her, her eyes widened as she envisaged herself running such a business. Vegetables and fodder—well, she supposed she could learn how to cope with that side of the smallholding, but pigs! She stared down at her small hands now twisted together in her lap, and swallowed hard as Doyle's scathing comments once again washed over her. She didn't mind growing fodder or vegetables, but keeping pigs was definitely out. She knew next to nothing about pig husbandry and was not inclined to become enlightened on this industry.

Her eyes took on a bleak look. It was too late now to stop and consider whether she had done the right thing in coming north. But she didn't have to stay, she argued silently with herself. If things got too tough then she could pull out, maybe sell the smallholding and take on another job such as companion to someone, or housekeeping. She took a deep breath. No sense in worrying about it until she had to. There was time enough to work out her future, as empty as it now seemed to her.

'I've been thinking,' said Clay, in a considering

tone, 'about that smallholding. It might be as well if it were sold off. It's up to you, of course. In any case, I suggest that you get a man in to do the heavy work until you've found your feet and decided what to do about it.'

Sheena looked at him. He had an uncanny way of reading her inner thoughts and she didn't like it, it put her at a disadvantage.

'Oh, I don't know about that,' she replied slowly, as if that would have been the last thing she would have contemplated. 'I don't mind hard work, and I've got to start somewhere and learn how to cope on my own.'

She received a swift hard look from Clay and sensed that she had displeased him, but she didn't mind that. She was grateful for what he had done for her father, and for bringing her back with him, but she didn't intend to be a burden to him. He had said that he was a busy man, hadn't he? He ought to be relieved that she was going to stand on her own two feet and not rely on others to cushion her from stark reality.

She stole a quick glance at his hard profile. He didn't look relieved, she thought—the opposite in fact. She hadn't, she reminded herself with a pang of remorse, thanked him for what he had done, and she ought not to have dismissed his advice quite so nonchalantly as she had done, even though it was sheer pique that had made her do so. 'Mr Dayman——' she began hesitantly, but Clay bit out at her, 'Clay's the name.'

This slightly threw her off her course, but she took a deep breath and began again. 'Clay,' she said firmly, 'I haven't thanked you for what you've done for my father, or for bringing me here—and I am grateful, believe me.' She hesitated a second, then added on a gentler note, 'And I will think about what you've advised. It's just that——' she stopped to search for the right words to convey her thoughts to him. 'When Dad left, I hadn't got a home, and I know I've been well looked after since then, but it wasn't home,' she said quietly. 'Now I've a chance to have a home again and it will be mine, and not some-one else's place.' She shook her head in a vague man-ner. 'I don't suppose any of this makes sense to you, and I'm not putting it very well. I suppose I just need time to settle down and think things out,' she ended lamely.

Clay guided the car off the main highway and on to a side road that wound up a slight incline. When they had got to the brow of the hill, he pulled in to the side of the road and looked ahead of him, and Sheena followed his glance.

She saw acres of paddocked land and set in the midst of the carefully tended gardens a large impos-ing-looking homestead built in the colonial style.

'That's Rimini,' he said, and Sheena took due note of the pride in his voice as he said the name.

'Rimini?' she repeated after him, thinking what an odd name it was.

'My grandfather was Italian, he named it after his home town in Italy,' Clay told her.

It took a second or so for Sheena to realise the sig-
nificance of what Clay had just said, and when it
did, her eyes widened. This was what he had described to Doyle as a 'holding of sorts'. She blinked.
No wonder he had wanted to take a swing at Doyle!
Barter's Ridge was no mean property, but this was on
an even grander scale.

In the far distance she saw cattle grazing, the dis-
tinctive colouring of the herd pronouncing that they
were Jerseys, and fine animals at that. So Clay Dayman was a dairy farmer, and a prosperous one by
all accounts. Doyle had wanted to try his hand at
dairy farming, Sheena recalled with a painful stab in
her heart region. He had often spoken of the possibility of changing from sheep to the dairying industry.

Sheena continued to gaze ahead of her, but her
eyes had misted over. Why had she to remember
things like that? It was no business of hers what
Doyle wanted, or had wanted in the past. It hadn't
concerned her for the past three years. She just had
to get out of the habit of thinking about him.

'This home you're looking forward to having might
come as a bit of a shock to you,' said Clay, abruptly
breaking into her miserable musings. 'It's a shack on
the eastern boundary of my property, and in dire
need of repair.'

He waited while she digested this news, then
added, 'I was hoping to persuade you to stay at
Rimini until other arrangements had been made.'

Sheena continued to look ahead of her, not wanting him to see the disappointment she had felt at his news. She hadn't expected a palace, she told herself stoutly. If her father had lived there, then surely it was habitable? She didn't mind roughing it. At least it would be hers, and she wouldn't be dependent on anyone's charity.

She blinked. Now what had made her think of her stay at Barter's Ridge as charity? She had paid for her board and lodging the only way she could. But it had been charity, and that was how she had looked at it deep within herself but would never have admitted it. She had spoken the truth when she had told Clay that she had never looked on Barter's Ridge as her home, and considering that she might have become Doyle's wife this was a strange paradox.

She glanced quickly at the silent man at her side now looking ahead of him. What manner of man was he? she wondered. She had told him things that she had not been able to admit to herself all the time she had stayed at Barter's Ridge. Whatever longings she had had, she had quashed them with fierce relentlessness, telling herself that she was lucky to have a roof over her head considering her father's treachery.

Her eyes turned towards the imposing homestead. She didn't belong there any more than she had belonged at Barter's Ridge, for surely her position would be the same, and she couldn't bear to go through all that again. As kind as Clay Dayman had been in offering her accommodation, she would still

feel like a stray kitten that he had picked up and felt
obliged to see to its welfare.

Her eyes left the homestead and rested on Clay,
who in spite of his apparent absorption on the view
in front of them was waiting for her reply. On recalling his annoyance when she had shown her independence earlier, she knew she had to be very
careful how she answered this latest suggestion of his.
'I wasn't expecting anything grand,' she said, managing to inject a light note into her voice. 'As long
as it's got a roof, I won't mind—honestly.' The last
word was added in a pleading manner, telling him
that she hoped that he understood.

If he did understand, there was no sign of it in his
forbidding features as he surveyed her coolly. His
dark eyes held an almost mesmeric hold upon her,
and it was all Sheena could do not to backtrack
hastily and say that she would be grateful and hon-
oured to stay at his home. The past was still fresh in
her mind, and that alone held her firm and her clear
blue gaze did not waver as she met his inscrutable
one.

'I admire your pioneering spirit,' he said dryly.
'However, I must confess to having an ulterior motive
in wanting your presence at the homestead.'

Sheena's eyes now took on a wary look. Were they
short of labour? she wondered, and experienced a
sudden shock of disappointment at the thought. She
had somehow thought Clay Dayman beyond such
machinations, but then her father had worked for
him, she reminded herself bleakly.

'There's Vicky, you see,' he said carefully. 'She's young, and she needs company.' His eyes left Sheena and he looked towards the homestead again. 'It's an all-male domain down there, I'm afraid, and although she's never said so, I'm pretty certain she'd welcome another female's company into the household.' He was silent for a second or so, then added, 'She's been under medical observation for almost six months now, and it curtails her social activities.'

Sheena looked quickly away from Clay. She could feel a net being placed slowly but irrevocably over her. To turn him down would sound not only ungrateful but extremely unkind. She presumed that Vicky was his wife and through her illness, whatever it was, she was unable to circulate amongst their friends. She was extremely sorry for her, but could hardly see what they would have in common should she succumb to this subtle blackmail he was using on her.

'Perhaps I could visit her,' she said, carefully avoiding those hypnotic eyes of his, and again experiencing a desperate wish to please him and utterly miserable because she couldn't. It was her future she was fighting for, and to give in now would be stupid. She mightn't get on with Vicky, and then where would she be? If she was Clay's wife, then instinctively Sheena knew she would be a very lovely woman, and no matter how kind she was, there would be times when she would be watching points where Sheena and Clay were concerned. It would only be natural, she thought wretchedly, and hardly a point she could raise for Clay's attention without causing herself some embarrassment.

Clay's deep resigned-sounding sigh, and his despondent, 'Very well,' before he started up the engine and glided the car down over the brow and towards the outer boundaries of his property was not lost on the miserable Sheena, and his calm acceptance of her refusal to co-operate with his plans made her fervently wish that he would take her straight to the smallholding and leave her there.

Soon it became apparent that they were not heading for the homestead but following a road that skirted it and out to an area well beyond the homestead precincts, and Sheena saw with no small relief that her unspoken wish was about to be fulfilled. He was taking her to the smallholding, she was sure of it.

A few miles further on, however, she was not so certain, as he drew up beside an enclosed area and motioned that she should get out and join him. Then he led her through a wicket gate and down a paved path.

When she realised that they were in a small enclosure that contained a graveyard, her steps faltered and she braced herself for the ordeal to come. Clay was taking her to her father's grave.

The newly dug grave lay at the end of the enclosure, and there was a plain wooden cross at its head. Someone had placed a small bouquet of wild flowers on the grave that now looked somehow forlorn as the sun had slightly withered them. 'The smallholding's only a mile further on,' commented Clay, 'but as we had to pass by here I thought you might like to visit.'

Sheena nodded in reply, but could not speak. She felt numb. She knew no grief, and she ought to have done. She had loved her father once, but his selfishness in taking something that didn't belong to him and causing her so much heartbreak had replaced that love with bitterness.

Her small hands clenched into fists by her side. She wanted to feel something and was astounded by her lack of emotion. It could be argued that the emotional storm that had suddenly erupted at the start of their journey north had left her spent of all emotion, but that didn't occur to her at the time, and she just stood looking at the grave.

'Shall we move on?' said Clay quietly, yet there was a note in his voice that held a certain amount of censure in it, and Sheena, following him out of the graveyard, was very much aware of it. Her non-reaction had surprised herself, and she could well understand Clay's thoughts on the matter. Perhaps one day she would see things in a different light. She didn't want to go on feeling bitter about the past.

CHAPTER FOUR

CLAY closed the car door behind her and shut it with a hard final snap, then got in the driver's seat and turned on the ignition, but did not move out on to the road again. 'You're finding it hard to forgive him, aren't you?' he said.

Sheena started, and stared at him. She didn't want to talk about it, but it seemed she didn't have much choice. She took a deep breath and looked back at the enclosed area they had just left. 'I can't understand why he did it. It was so stupid,' she replied in a low voice. 'It's not so much that I can't forgive— at least, I don't think so,' she added in a weary voice.

'Lots of us do stupid things,' answered Clay. 'They could be called blind spots, when we act typically out of character, but there's always a reason for what we do, even if it's wrong.'

Sheena looked back at him and her blue eyes were shadowed. 'Why didn't he write to me? And why didn't he tell Doyle where the money was, and apologise?' she asked in a low voice. 'It could have——' she broke off lamely. There was no point in going on. It was over, finished with.

'Made a difference where you and Charter were concerned?' asked Clay, finishing her sentence for her and making a deep flush appear on her cheeks.

'From what I saw of Charter, I'm of the opinion that it wouldn't have made any difference if he had,' he added darkly. 'The return of the money didn't either, did it?' he queried sarcastically.

Sheena's hands clenched into fists so tightly that she could feel the point of her nails biting into her palms. What business was it of his? she asked herself bitterly. Why couldn't he leave her alone? Thank goodness she had turned his proposition down. He would be sure to discuss all this with his wife, and she would find herself having to accept unwanted advice from that quarter too.

Her set lips and proud lift of her head as she looked straight ahead of her said more than words. She wanted them to be on their way. She was tired, but more than this, she needed to be alone.

'Did it ever occur to you that your father was an exceedingly unhappy man?' said Clay, totally ignoring her wish that they should leave. 'I didn't know much about him when he first came looking for work, but I did know that he needed help, and I'm not talking about material needs.'

Sheena gave a light shrug as if to say that if he was unhappy, then it was entirely his own fault.

'I didn't probe into his past, and I didn't seek any references,' went on Clay steadily. 'It was fairly obvious that he expected to be turned down, but had to ask anyway. It's my guess that he'd sought work all the way up the coast, and received short shrift for his trouble. He hadn't used a penny of that money, remember, so he couldn't have had much on him by the time he got this far. Well, I took him on, and I never regretted my decision. I liked your father, Sheena, and knowing what I now know about his past, I would still like him, and I respect the kind of man he was.'

With that he put his foot on the accelerator and guided the car on to the road again. 'He once told me he'd been a fool,' he said slowly, persisting with the subject that Sheena had hoped would be dropped now that they were on their way to the smallholding. 'He said he didn't know why he'd done what he had, only that something had happened that had made his present existence intolerable. He said he ought to have seen it coming, and when it did, he couldn't take it.'

He glanced at Sheena out of the corner of his eye. 'Do you know what that was?' he queried softly, and when she said nothing he added, 'I think it was your engagement to Doyle Charter.'

This brought a quick reaction from the hitherto silent Sheena, who gave a gasp and said indignantly, 'It couldn't have been! He was really pleased about it, he said——' She faltered as she recalled her father's last words to her and how she hadn't been able to understand the meaning behind what he had said—not until the next morning, when it all became painfully clear.

'Well?' queried Clay mildly, waiting for her to go on.

'Oh, nothing,' replied Sheena wearily.

'You've remembered something, haven't you?' persisted Clay.

'I don't want to talk about it!' Sheena exclaimed on a note of sheer desperation. 'Can't you see that? Don't you think I haven't tried to make excuses for what he did? He had a good job with good wages. I made him comfortable and looked after him, just as Mum would have done if she'd still been with us. I know he felt her loss more than he'd ever let on.' She swallowed. 'He used to say as long as we were together, we'd get by—and we did,' she ended on a cracked note.

Clay nodded. 'Well, just keep thinking on those lines,' he said quietly, 'and perhaps you'll see things from a different point of view. You were all he had, remember. And for your sake he hadn't allowed himself to grieve for his wife. It might have been better if he had.'

After this he fell silent and concentrated on his driving, and Sheena just looked ahead of her out of the window, hating him for bringing back the past with such painful clarity. She knew he was right, but she hadn't the will or the spirit to accept his advice. Tomorrow perhaps, or the next day—who knew?

Sheena's first sight of her father's smallholding was not a comforting one. As she gazed over the roughly erected fencing that enclosed the property and saw the almost derelict-looking area in front of her, it was of no comfort to tell herself that her father's illness must have caused him to neglect the property. That crops had grown there and very probably produced a good harvest was hard to imagine, and she felt a lump rise in her throat. Doyle must have had second sight, she thought, for his descrip-

tion had been uncannily near the mark. It did look a
rundown property.

When she followed Clay's tall figure through an
iron gate and skirted the growing area through a
rough beaten-down track, there was worse to come
as her depressed gaze took in what had once been a
wooden shack on the edge of the property, but now
was nothing but a heap of old timber that had obviously come under a demolition order.

Clay's quick, 'My, my!' did nothing to alleviate
the fury Sheena felt building up inside her. Someone
had knocked that shack down, that much was plain,
and whoever it was they would have to make good
the damage, she thought furiously. Her temper turned
to utter frustration when she realised that there was
absolutely no chance of her living there, or indeed
anywhere on the smallholding as the ruin she was
staring at was, or had been, the only building in
sight.

'It appears that they got to work a little earlier
than I anticipated,' said Clay, casting an apologetic
look at her.

Sheena turned and stared at him. 'You mean you
ordered the shack to be knocked down?' she asked
him incredulously.

He gave her another apologetic look. 'Not exactly,'
he said mildly. 'I did give orders for some repairs to
be carried out before our arrival.'

Sheena was just about to take a deep breath and
ask him what he meant by interfering with what was
now her property, when a car was heard to draw up

and they turned their attention back to the road. An oldish-looking car had parked beside Clay's gleaming one and an elderly man got out, and giving Clay a quick salute from the distance came to join them. 'Dayee, boss,' the man addressed Clay, and stared at the demolished shack. 'Jim said weren't much he could do—place was falling down as it was. Reckoned it was safer to finish the job.' He looked at Sheena, his pale blue eyes showing curiosity.

'This is James Greig's daughter, Sam,' introduced Clay. 'Sheena, this is Sam Whitelaw. He used to work with your father, and he's now taken over as manager.'

As Sheena's small hand was lost in the big horny hand of Sam Whitelaw, she knew a sense of desolation. In spite of the man's kindly welcome and obvious wish to make her feel welcome, she was among strangers. Her look was bleak as she tried to echo his sincere wish that she 'took to the North, and made her home there.' She then looked beyond him at the ruined shack. 'I was hoping to move in today,' she said in a small voice, that told more of her disappointment to the watching men than she realised.

'I guess it wouldn't take more than a month for the boys to fix you up with a replacement,' Clay said carefully. 'Get on with it, will you, Sam?' he ordered quietly.

'Sure, boss,' replied Sam, directing a puzzled glance at Sheena and back again at Clay.

'Sheena's a mind to try and make a go of the busi-

ness,' Clay told him in answer to his unspoken query,
yet there was something in the careful way that he
had offered the information that made Sheena give
him a hard look.

He didn't believe that she was capable of running
such a business, she thought, but she would show
him, and his manager, Sam, who appeared to be of
the same opinion, if his doubtful look was anything
to go by.

She stared around her. She could see no sign of the
pigs, and for that she was grateful. Clay must have
had them removed elsewhere to be looked after,
after her father's death.

A thought then struck her that made her bite on
her lower lip hard. Not once had she shown any interest in how her father had died. She had just
accepted the fact and taken it from there, yet he had
only been in his early fifties. 'Did——' she swallowed, and started again, forcing herself to ask the
question. 'Did my father have a long illness?' she
asked, for some reason directing her question at Sam.

Sam swept off his broad-brimmed hat that he had
donned again after his introduction to Sheena, and
wiped his dark sunburned forehead. 'Guess he must
have,' he replied cogitatingly. 'One minute he was
carrying on much as usual, the next——' he did not
finish the sentence but glanced towards Clay for help.

'He had to give up full-time work a year ago,' said
Clay. 'That's why he took up this smallholding. He
didn't say much about what was wrong with him
when he asked to be relieved of his job, but I guessed

that whatever was wrong, it had to be serious enough for him to start to take life quietly. I know who his doctor was, and I'm sure that he'll fill in the details for you later.'

Sheena turned her glance away from them with an abrupt movement. He had been ill—must have been for months, yet he had never told her, or sent for her. Her teeth gritted on the thought. He had thought her happily married to Doyle, and it had been too late when he had discovered the truth.

'I'm afraid you'll have to accept my offer after all,' said Clay with a quiet firmness, and caught her arm gently below her elbow and turned her round towards the road again. There was a kind of possessiveness about that touch that puzzled Sheena, but she was in no mood to contest it. She just wanted to get away from this forlorn area where her father had lived out the last days of his life, too proud to ask for help, from her or anyone.

It wasn't until she was sitting in the car waiting for Clay to finish whatever he was telling Sam and join her prior to taking her to his home that the suspicion entered her mind and began to take a firm hold on her.

From Sam Whitelaw's reaction it was plain that he had never expected her to take on where her father had left off. Clay's reaction had been the same, only he had been a little more reserved in keeping his opinions to himself. However, it seemed that he had got it all planned. Even if they had not knocked the shack down, the work that would have had to be done on it would have necessitated her finding temporary lodging until the work was completed. Yet he had said nothing of this when she had stated her preference for a home of her own.

Her lips folded tightly. His wife needed a companion, and Miss Sheena Greig admirably filled the post—in his eyes anyway, she thought bitterly. She smoothed back a wandering stray of hair. Well, she was very sorry, but when that shack was completed she intended moving into it come what may, and no amount of persuasion would deter her from her course.

CHAPTER FIVE

ON the way to Rimini Clay, well aware of Sheena's keen disappointment, wisely made no comment on the state of the land or the demolition of what she had hoped would be her home.

From Sheena's point of view this was just as well, for had he attempted to make any soothing comments she might have said something that she would later regret, since in all honesty this silent man at her side had tried to do his best for her, even though he had had an ulterior motive.

Within a remarkably short space of time the car was slowing to a stop at the rear of the homestead beside some outbuildings. One was a large double garage, and on the opposite side of the wide yard were the stables.

There was an air of old-fashioned stability about the whole area. The buildings were well cared for as were the grounds surrounding the homestead, and as Sheena followed Clay to the back entrance of the homestead her eye caught several more buildings away to her right. These were enclosed in a white fenced-off section and were plainly the dairy quarters of the farm, for the paddocks with the grazing animals that Sheena had seen from a distance lay alongside.

The homestead was far away enough from the dairy to ensure its privacy from the bustle of the milking scene. Sheena felt a small spurt of envy towards the Dayman family, even though she acknowledged the fact that much hard work and effort had gone into making the property as fine as it was.

As they approached the wide verandah that ran the length of the back premises a little girl erupted out of a cane chair, scattering a pile of magazines in several directions, and hurled herself at Clay.

'You didn't say!' she accused him, as she pushed her dark curly head into his chest and clung to him, with what seemed to Sheena a fierce intensity.

Clay extricated himself gently from the fervent embrace and took the child's hand in his. 'Vicky, this is Sheena. She's staying with us for a spell.' He looked at Sheena. 'This is Vicky, Sheena. She will no doubt enliven your stay with us.' He looked back at the child now studying Sheena with a wary expression in her large dark eyes. 'Vicky, take Sheena to the room next to yours,' he ordered.

Sheena took particular note of the way that Vicky's eyes now took on a speculative look as against the previous wary one, and she had an uncomfortable feeling that she knew what she was thinking and wondered if her father, for Clay must be her father since there was a family likeness between them, was in the habit of bringing home lady visitors at a moment's notice.

It seemed that Vicky had finished her summing-up of Sheena, and liked what she saw, for she held out a small hand towards her. 'How do you do,' she said in a stilted well-practised voice that made Clay smile, showing those strong white teeth of his.

'Bring Sheena down to the kitchen when she's ready,' he told Vicky. 'Like me, I expect she's starving. I'll go and see what Pietro can rustle up for us.'

With Vicky's hand in hers, Sheena allowed herself to be taken into the homestead. As the child chattered on about nothing in particular, mainly Sheena suspected, to give herself time to accustom herself to this sudden invasion of a stranger, Sheena wondered how old she was, and thought she was probably around the ten to twelve mark. She also wondered where her mother was, whether she was in hospital at that particular time, or in her room resting.

Clay had said nothing about the child, she thought puzzledly, only mentioning an invalid who must be his wife. It was not uncommon to name the daughter after the mother. On recalling what he had said about Vicky needing a companion, she presumed that the child was sent to a boarding school, in which case she ought to be still at school. Sheena gave up all speculation on this thought. She would just have to wait for the answers.

The inside of the homestead was in keeping with the rest of the property, and again Sheena sensed an age-old permanency about the well-furnished rooms. This was a family home and had a warmth about it that not even the fine furnishings could dispel, for first and foremost it was a home, and would always be.

'This is your room. How long are you staying?' asked Vicky, as she flung open a door on the first floor landing and stood politely aside for Sheena to enter first.

'About a month, maybe less,' replied Sheena, gazing about her and taking due note of the well-furnished room with its single divan and beautifully embroidered quilt. 'It all depends how long it takes to build another——' Here she paused, wondering what the child would think if she knew just what sort of a home Sheena was waiting to go into. A wider comparison between Rimini and the home of Sheena's father would be hard to find—'Home,' she added slowly, not wanting to say 'shack' and arouse the child's curiosity. She had enough to cope with with Clay's well-meant advice without raising more questions on the subject.

'Have you lost your home?' asked the child, gazing at Sheena with earnest sympathy.

Sheena gave an inward sigh. How did she answer that? 'Well,' she replied carefully, 'it just needs re-building. When it's ready, I shall move in.' She looked pointedly at her watch. 'I'd love a shower, could you show me where the bathroom is?' she asked Vicky, thus forestalling any further discussion on this point.

Vicky was instantly contrite. 'Clay would wallop me if he knew I'd kept you talking,' she said, with a small smile that belied her words. 'It's two doors down, across the passage, I'll show you,' and she led the way for a slightly shocked Sheena to follow her.

Sheena had never called her father by his christian name, and although some parents preferred this form of address, it didn't sound right to her.

After a quick shower she felt a little more able to cope with what looked like a very frustrating few weeks until she could go back to the smallholding.

When she got back to her room she found Vicky sitting on her bed and her cases stacked beside the large wardrobe. 'Do you want to change before we go down?' Vicky asked as she watched Sheena towelling her hair dry. 'Clay brought your cases up,' she added.

Sheena looked down at her blouse and jeans, which were still fresh-looking, then looked back at Vicky who was also wearing a similar outfit. 'I always wear jeans,' Vicky answered with a grin, replying to Sheena's unspoken question. 'Mummy's always on about it, but she doesn't mind really. It's just that she's a fashion model. I have to dress up whenever we have a party, of course,' she added thoughtfully.

Sheena's hand that was vigorously rubbing her hair with the towel suddenly stilled and she blinked. 'A fashion model?' she queried carefully, hoping that the surprise she felt at this news did not show through to the child.

Vicky nodded vigorously and there was pride in her voice as she said, 'One of the top ones too. There's some magazines downstairs with her picture in, I'll show you them later.'

Sheena continued rubbing her hair dry, but her thoughts were on the child. It was obvious that

Vicky did not know that her mother was ill, and this was most odd, for surely she would have said something about her mother having to give up work. She sighed inwardly. It rather sounded as if Mrs Dayman's illness was serious enough to be kept from the child, and Sheena would have to be very careful in what she said. 'I suppose her life is very much like a film star's,' she said casually, 'and now she's taking a nice rest from publicity.'

Vicky's friendly attitude suddenly changed to an antagonistic one and she glared at Sheena. 'No, she's not!' she replied vehemently. 'She's with Dad in Paraguay. He's a photographer and takes most of Mummy's pictures. He's good too,' she added on a wistful note. 'They usually take me with them when they go abroad, but I had a rotten exam to sit for and couldn't go with them.'

Her attitude changed back to a friendly one. 'You'll like them,' she said confidingly. 'Everyone does, and although I like being with Clay, I shall be glad when they get back.'

A little light pierced through the darkness surrounding Sheena. 'Clay's your uncle, then?' she asked, taking a stab in the dark as she remembered him telling her of his family.

'Course!' replied Vicky a trifle indignantly, as if to say that everyone knew that.

'Lunch is on the table!' Clay called up to them from somewhere down below, and Sheena hastily put a comb through her hair and after a quick look to see if it was tidy, joined Vicky at the door and went downstairs.

Considering that the meal was supposed to be an impromptu one she was surprised at the assortment of food placed on the table. There were cooked meats, breast of cold chicken sliced in generous portions and side salad.

Clay had changed into a light blue shirt and denims, and Sheena was a little sorry that she had not changed too, but Vicky's presence eased any worry she might have had in that direction.

Despite the fact that Vicky must have had lunch not much above an hour before Clay and Sheena had theirs, she sat down and tucked in with them, much to Clay's amusement, and in between mouthfuls of chicken, wanted to know where Clay had been for the last two days.

Clay told her about the cattle sales he had attended before going south. He looked at Sheena. 'Sheena is Mr Greig's daughter, Vicky, and she's going to live up here.'

Vicky nodded complacently at this. 'She's having a house built, she told me.'

Sheena looked hastily down at her plate, not wanting to meet Clay's eyes. She hadn't actually said it was a house, but then she hadn't said it was a shack either.

'Well,' replied Clay carefully, 'it's not exactly the kind of place I'd want her to settle in,' and at Sheena's quick look at him with blue fire in her eyes, he went on casually, 'I mean, I think she'll find it lonely on her own. I've tried to persuade her to stay on with us. You'll have to see what you can do about it.'

'I've already explained to your uncle how I feel about that,' replied the fuming Sheena. There was nothing like having things put on the line. Any minute now he would probably give the child the whole miserable history behind her move to the North, and that she couldn't bear.

'There's plenty of time yet,' replied Clay with a certain inflection of purpose in his voice that worried Sheena.

Vicky looked from Sheena to Clay and back at Sheena again. 'I'm not staying either,' she said, darting what Sheena could only interpret as a defiant look at Clay. 'When my mother and father...'

'Vicky!' thundered Clay, and there was no mistaking the warning note in his voice.

'They will too!' Vicky flung back at him with what seemed to Sheena to be unnecessary fury, and leapt out of her chair and ran out of the kitchen.

Sheena stared at the slammed door, then back at Clay who was looking in the same direction with narrowed eyes. At this point another door opened at the back of them and a small dark wiry-haired man entered, carrying a pot of coffee and a jug of cream which he placed on the table. 'Tantrums?' he said, more as a statement than a question.

Clay nodded abruptly. 'You'd better take her a drink and a couple of tablets, Pietro.' He then looked at Sheena. 'This is Pietro, Sheena—cook, and man of all trades. If you want to know anything and I'm not around, ask Pietro.' His hard expression relaxed for a second as he added, 'He's been with the family for more years than either of us care to remember, eh, Pietro?' His face resumed its hard expression as he said, 'This is James Greig's daughter, Pietro. She's staying for a spell.'

There was nothing said here about hoping that Sheena would make the stay permanent, and Sheena wondered if he had at last relinquished the idea, but she didn't know him well enough to be certain of this. As for the little scene that had taken place a few moments before Pietro's entrance, she was mystified.

As she took the small man's hand in hers, and listened to his rather embarrassed sentiments on the death of her father, she couldn't help feeling a little sorry for Clay Dayman. It appeared that he not only had a sick wife on **his** hands, but a niece with quick-silver emotions liable to erupt at a moment's notice. She had not liked the reference to tablets, and was of the opinion that the good old-fashioned remedies were more in keeping with such behaviour. However, she was hardly in a position to point this out.

After Pietro had left there was a short silence in the room, and Sheena wondered if Clay would now suggest that she meet his wife, although Vicky had made no mention of her aunt. In all probability, Sheena mused, she had fallen out with her too, par-ticularly when she recalled the way Vicky had glared at her in the bedroom for what seemed to be very little reason.

She watched Clay pour out their coffee and was reminded of the very same scene before their journey north, and this brought her thoughts back to Doyle, and she wished it hadn't. She would have to let him know that she was settled. A lump rose in her throat at the thought, and she swallowed quickly as she accepted the coffee from Clay and felt him glance at her with those too-knowing eyes of his.

To cover her feelings and not give away her thoughts, she said quickly, 'Is your wife——'

'I have no wife,' Clay broke in abruptly, his dark eyes relentlessly noting Sheena's embarrassment. 'I believe I did say that this was an all-male domain. Vicky's the only female here.'

Sheena's embarrassment turned to puzzlement and she gave Clay an accusing look. 'But Vicky's not sick,' she said. 'She's a normal, healthy girl.' Her smooth forehead creased into a frown as she sought for the right words. 'So she has tantrums, but that's probably due to her age. What is she? I'd put her about eleven or twelve,' she went on, answering her own question. 'She's just growing up, and there's no doubt that she misses her mother and father.'

'What did she say about them when you were alone?' Clay cut in before she could finish her summing-up.

Sheena gave him an exasperated look. 'Only the usual sort of things a child says,' she replied patiently. 'That her mother was a fashion model and that her father was a photographer,' she gave a light shrug. 'Even if it wasn't true—well, what does it matter? They're only daydreams.'

Clay's eyes left Sheena and fastened on a spot behind her, but he was not seeing the kitchen wall, and there was a look in his eye that she could not interpret.

'Vicky's fifteen,' he said with quiet deliberation. 'As for daydreams—well, you didn't know it, but you hit the nail on the head there. Her parents were what she said they were, but were is the operative word. They never reached Paraguay, their plane came down in dense forest only a few miles from their destination. There were no survivors.'

It took a second or so for Sheena to grasp the stark implication of his words, and when it did, her eyes widened in consternation. She stared back at Clay. 'You mean, she doesn't know they died in the crash?' she asked in a shocked voice as she envisaged Vicky's reaction to the news.

Clay's eyes went back to the spot on the wall again before he answered harshly, 'She knows, only she won't accept it. That's what I meant by daydreams. She's put up a mental block of defence against the truth. You saw her reaction just then, didn't you? It's the same each time we try to get through to her.'

Sheena looked down at the floor, noting absently how flawlessly clean the bright parquet tiles were, but her thoughts were not on Pietro's domestic abilities. She had been just fifteen when she had lost her mother, and she could recall only too well the loss and the resultant grief of that loss. But she had not been alone, her father had been there to console her —a father who had laid his personal grief aside in order to comfort his daughter. She blinked hastily. Vicky had lost her father too. She shook her head bewilderedly. It didn't seem right that she should lose both parents.

'If there's anything I can do, I shall be glad to do it,' she said in a low voice, and looked swiftly away from Clay who was now watching her closely. 'I lost my mother when I was the same age,' she added quietly, 'so I know how it feels.'

'But you had your father, didn't you?' Clay reminded her, a little cruelly to Sheena's way of thinking, nevertheless it was the truth and she nodded dumbly in acknowledgment of this.

'Then you'll stay on?' Clay asked her abruptly, making it look as if she had a choice, though she had a nasty feeling that she hadn't.

'Until Vicky gets straightened out,' she replied cautiously, not wanting to commit herself further.

'That might be for a very long time,' Clay warned her. 'She's kept up this charade for almost six months.' At Sheena's surprised gasp, he gave a grim nod. 'I did tell you that she was receiving medical help, didn't I? Well, the specialist's advice was not to rush it. He's convinced that she'll come out of it in her own good time.'

'But surely,' began Sheena in a puzzled voice, 'surely her friends and other people know the truth,' she hesitated. 'I mean, how can she possibly keep up such a pretence?'

'By attacking anyone who dares to attempt to break down the barrier she's erected,' Clay replied. 'It's just as well that she's at an age when we can dispense with further schooling. If she'd been younger

I would have had to get in a tutor. She's in no state to mix with other girls of her own age. In their own line her parents were quite well known. There was a splash in the papers about the tragedy at the time, and her blatant refusal to acknowledge their deaths would only make her a target for well-meaning but entirely misguided do-gooders.'

Sheena thought about this aspect, but she couldn't really agree with the diagnosis. 'It's got to happen some time,' she said quietly. 'She's got to admit to the truth one day—I would have thought the sooner the better. The longer it goes on, the harder it's going to be for her to accept.'

Clay's well-moulded mouth hardened. 'It's not as easy as that,' he said grimly. 'Two months before the crash my mother, Vicky's grandmother, died. If there was anyone Vicky loved as much as she loved her parents, it was her gran, and she took it hard. She's an emotional child,' he went on in a weary voice. 'You must have noticed that much. She was brought up in an atmosphere of love and stability, now she has nothing but a huge emotional void in her life, and it's that that she can't accept. She needs stability and understanding, and that's what I'm trying to provide for her.'

Sheena watched Clay's long lean fingers suddenly curl into a hard fist, and again she felt the strength of the man and wondered why he hadn't married. Men of his looks and calibre, apart from his obvious wealth, were rarities not often encountered. In that way he reminded her of Doyle, and she was sure that many a feminine glance had been directed hopefully in his direction. She was also sure that he was not a man to play the field, not after he had fixed his sights on the woman that he had decided to marry. That was just the way that Sheena saw it. He would go singleminded after his prey and would brook no refusal. She had already had some experience of this singlemindedness of his where she was concerned, and could well imagine the forces that would be brought into being where his personal hopes were concerned. The woman wouldn't stand a chance!

Clay's voice broke into her musings, making a slight flush stain her cheeks, and she was fervently grateful that his thoughts were elsewhere and he was not likely to pick up her wayward ones. 'Vicky could have gone to one of my other sisters' homes. They were quite willing to take her, but they've children of their own, and right now I feel that the comparison to their happy existence as against her empty one would be more than she could take. Later perhaps it might be a good idea, but not now.'

Sheena nodded in agreement with this observation. 'It's a pity that she hasn't any brothers or sisters,' she commented thoughtfully, 'especially if they'd been a lot younger than herself—she would have rallied round then and had no time to brood.'

Clay's thoughtful eyes rested on her. 'She needs a diversion right enough, I'll agree with you there, and I'm hoping that between us we can provide one.'

Her solemn eyes met his. 'We can try anyway,' she replied quietly.

Clay smiled at her, and she felt a sharp pull at her heart strings that somewhat surprised her, but she put her reactions down to the unexpectedness of that sudden smile. 'Good!' he replied with evident satisfaction. 'I was hoping you'd feel that way. Firstly, I suggest that we get to know each other a little better. The news of our engagement won't then be shown in the light of a ploy to break down Vicky's defences— which it will be, of course,' he added, with no small amount of amusement in his eyes as he took in Sheena's shocked expression.

Sheena blinked. She felt like shaking her head. She hadn't heard right, surely? Was she mad, or was he? Nothing had been said about an engagement, even a mock one. She gave him a look of sheer exasperation and on seeing the wicked imp of amusement still lurking in those dark eyes of his, she swallowed. 'I don't feel I can promise you that much support,' she said in a voice that had lost its natural tone.

She was now coming out of shock, and as the whole, to her mind, absurd situation loomed up before her, she added furiously, 'I don't think it's funny! In fact, it's ridiculous! And you know it!' she tacked on fervently. 'For goodness' sake, where did you get such an absurd idea from?' she queried on a distracted note.

Clay's eyes went over her slight figure in a slow appraising manner and Sheena felt herself flush, and she wanted to slap his arrogant face. She supposed she ought to have been flattered by his suggestion, but he had forgotten Doyle. She loved Doyle and wanted no entanglement with any other man—mock or otherwise.

His eyes came to rest on her bright cheeks and then took in her sparkling eyes that now gleamed like blue sapphires. 'Now that's a silly thing to say,' he drawled lightly, making her flush deepen in embarrassment. 'As a matter of fact,' he went on in a calm voice, 'I've had the idea for,' he glanced at his watch, 'just over twenty-four hours.'

Sheena took in a deep breath to calm herself. Before they had left for the North was what he meant. Had her precipitate arrival the evening before, in what he had described as a disarrayed state, given him the idea? Was he now about to adopt the same kind of tactic that he thought Doyle had adopted? Was she, in his eyes, fair game? Being engaged to her would give him the right to her company at all times —and not only that, she thought with a stab of sheer panic as she envisaged him making affectionate advances towards her.

Her dark hair bounced from side to side, as she said emphatically, 'Well, you'll just have to forget it. I'll help any other way, but not that way.'

'Not even to cure a sick girl?' Clay asked gently, but with a touch of challenge in his voice that Sheena tried hard to ignore. 'You know it could have useful side effects,' he continued lightly. 'While I appreciate your feelings in not wanting to get involved, at least, not in that particular way, there's nothing like competition for settling an issue one way or the other. You know what I'm talking about, don't you?' he asked quietly. 'It won't cost you anything either. I have no intention of overstepping our present relationship. You don't have to believe me, of course, but I'd like you to give it a try.'

His gaze left Sheena and he gazed back at the wall behind her again. 'It was a little game Vicky used to play with my mother when she came to stay with us. Mother was a great matchmaker. After the girls married, she turned her attention on John and me, and we were holding our own,' he commented with a wry smile, 'until John decided to take the plunge a year ago. That left me in the hot seat as far as the matrimonial stakes went, particularly as I was older than John.' He gave an expressive shrug. 'It was a family joke, you see, all perfectly harmless, but Vicky entered into it with as much enthusiasm as Mother did.'

His gaze returned suddenly to the watching Sheena, who still had a wary look in her eye. 'I'm just asking you to help me get her back to normal. I know that to your way of thinking what I've suggested sounds a very odd way of doing it, but believe me, it's the very thing to lift her out of her world of makebelieve.'

'By presenting her with another makebelieve situation?' Sheena queried sceptically. 'I don't see how that's going to help, particularly when she finds out the truth. You'll be back to square one with a vengeance then,' she warned him.

Clay gave her an odd kind of assessing look that she could make nothing of, but it disturbed her somehow. As a possible interpretation hit her she drew in her breath sharply. He could be telling her that it might not be a makebelieve situation. She expelled her breath slowly. If that was so then she had better make a few things clear right from the start.

She was about to expound on this when Clay beat her to it with a casual, 'Remember what I said about it having useful side effects? As for Vicky having a relapse, I very much doubt that she would—either way, it's a diversion that I can't afford to pass up. In spite of the specialist's advice, I feel that things have gone on long enough, and I'm sure you'll agree with me there,' he added significantly.

Sheena was still thinking about his remark about the useful side effects of such a situation and was only too well aware of what he was referring to. The way he saw it was that it would make Doyle come up to scratch. He had also mentioned something about competition and how there was nothing like it to settle an issue. She swallowed convulsively. She didn't want Doyle on those terms. He'd had plenty of chances to make the past up to her but he hadn't taken one of them, not even after the money had been returned. Her lips firmed. Doyle didn't want to marry her, at last not legally. He wanted her to be his common-law wife. Her soft lips twisted ironically at the thought—it was a nicer way of putting it than the old term of 'mistress'.

She suspected that this hard man watching her with a close scrutiny was well aware of Doyle's true intentions where she was concerned. He'd called him a heel, hadn't he? Yet for his own convenience he was willing to forget all his previous deductions on this front, even to the point of lowering his haughty standards and holding out a chance of a re-union between her and Doyle as bait to gain her co-operation. Sheena closed her eyes. She didn't know what she had done to deserve landing herself in such a predicament.

'I'm not quite sure what you mean by useful side effects,' she replied coldly, not caring if he knew that she was lying, and judging by the way that his eyes narrowed, he did. 'But if you're referring to Mr Charter, I have no intention of letting him know where I'm staying—at least,' she amended hastily, as she realised that this bald statement left her completely without a genuine excuse to go back to the south should she ever wish to do so, and the way things were going it looked as if she might need such an excuse, 'until I'm ready to do so,' she ended lamely. 'I am really sorry but I can't agree to what you've suggested.' She felt very mean as she said this. Clay had done a lot for her and she hated not being able to comply with his wishes. If he'd asked anything else of her she would be only too pleased to help.

He did not reply but stood looking at her, and she began to feel mesmerised, as if by sheer will power alone he was trying to force her to do what he wanted her to do. In sheer desperation she cried out, 'Surely there's someone more suitable than me to ask to carry out that role? I'm sure you've lots of friends——' She hesitated here; she had wanted to say girl-friends but had said friends, but he must know what she meant, she thought crossly.

A sardonic smile appeared on Clay's face as he replied dryly, 'I'm not short of feminine company, if that's what you're referring to,' making her blush and feel as if she had spoken out of turn. 'The trouble is,' he went on slowly, but deliberately, 'that charming as they may be, I have no intention of putting my neck in that kind of noose, not even a makebelieve one.'

Sheena looked away. She knew what he meant. He wasn't boasting, just stating a bald fact. That he was considered a matrimonial prize came as no surprise to her. She could also understand why he had chosen her as the fictional fiancée. He would be safe with her because he knew that she loved Doyle. She stared down at her hands now twisted together tightly. It was little enough to do for him surely, and she did owe him some allegiance for what he had done for her father. She looked up slowly and met Clay's enigmatic gaze. 'Very well,' she said in a low voice, and gave a helpless shrug. 'If you really think it will help,' she added lamely.

Clay's sober expression vanished as she spoke, and he gave her a heartstopping smile that made her hold her breath for a second and wonder just what she had let herself in for. 'Thank you, Sheena,' he said quietly, 'I had a feeling I could rely on you.'

CHAPTER SIX

DIRECTLY after lunch, Clay suggested that Sheena might like to rest for the remainder of the afternoon, and this she gladly agreed to. So much had happened during the short period of time since her arrival at Rimini that a rest, or a peaceful interlude, was of dire necessity.

As she made her way to the room that Vicky had taken her to earlier, she felt like a long-distance runner. She was breathless and utterly depleted, as if she had run the distance from the South to the North and was now ready for a well-earned rest.

She kicked off her sandals and with a sigh of thankfulness sank down on to the bed and as soon as her head had touched the pillows she was sound asleep.

When she awoke it was dusk, and it took her some time to get her bearings. When she had them she sat up quickly, wondering what time it was and how long she had slept.

Other things then impinged upon her, such as the astounding suggestion made by Clay that they should enter into a mock engagement in order to divert Vicky from carrying on with her pathetic make-believe that her parents were still alive.

'Are you awake?' asked a small tentative voice, as

the door opened and Vicky walked softly into the room as if not to disturb Sheena had she still been asleep.

'Just,' replied Sheena, accustoming her eyes to Vicky's dim outline as it was now almost dark. 'What time is it, Vicky?' she asked as she swung her legs off the bed and put on the bedside light.

'Four-thirty,' replied Vicky. 'I looked in on you several times, but you were fast asleep. I suppose it's the travelling. I always got tired when we used to go abroad.'

Sheena looked back at Vicky, whose hair looked in need of a comb through, but did not comment on this. She wondered if she was going to carry on with her game of makebelieve, and if so, what she ought to do about it.

She was saved the necessity by Vicky suddenly asking, 'Are you Clay's girl-friend?'

Sheena gasped and stared back at Vicky, who met her astonished gaze with a look of limpid innocence, and Sheena, not knowing her well enough to be able to tell whether it was feigned or not, replied cautiously, 'I'm not sure what you mean by that.'

Vicky shook her head impatiently. 'You know what I mean!' she asserted firmly. 'Clay's got lots of girl-friends, but he's never put them up in this room —so I kinda thought...' She hesitated as if searching for the right words.

Sheena gazed round the room slowly. 'What's so special about this room?' she asked curiously, breaking into Vicky's musings.

Vicky's small features seemed to close up for a second before she replied in what she tried hard to sound like a casual way, 'It was Grandma's.'

That was all she said, but it said a great deal more to Sheena than Vicky realised. Did she resent the fact that Clay had put her in her beloved grandmother's room? Sheena wondered. If she did, then it would not have been a very clever move on his part, particularly as he wanted Vicky to get on with her.

'Well, are you?' repeated Vicky impatiently, going back to her original question.

Sheena gave an inward sigh of exasperation. There was nothing like being thrown head first into the fray, she thought ironically. She got up from the bed and walked over to the ornate dressing table and started to lay out her brush and comb set on the inlaid top in order to give herself time to reply.

If she said that she was Clay's girl-friend, what then? Surely Vicky would have the intelligence to see through such a statement. She knew very well that Sheena had only met her uncle recently—very recently—twenty-four hours ago, to be exact, she recalled Clay's words on that same subject. At this thought a light flush stained her features and she hurriedly bent down pretending to look for something in the dressing table drawers so that her features were hidden from the watching Vicky. She then recalled what Clay had said about them having time to get acquainted before springing the 'engagement' on Vicky.

Her mind made up, she looked up at Vicky. 'No,

Vicky,' she replied steadily, hoping that she would not press the point.

'Then why did you take so long to answer?' asked the embarrassingly astute Vicky.

'Because I was slightly thrown by the question,' replied Sheena exasperatedly. 'I've only just met your uncle, as you well know. I didn't exactly expect to be asked such a question,' she tacked on for good measure.

Vicky gave her a wicked grin, but made no apology. 'Well, you soon will be,' she replied, almost nonchalantly, but with conviction.

Sheena stared at her. 'What if I had a boy-friend?' she asked lightly yet curiously, since it was the truth even though Vicky was not to know it.

Vicky gave an exaggerated shrug. 'That won't make any difference,' she told Sheena. 'You don't know Clay. I do, and if he wants you to be his girl-friend then you'll be his girl-friend,' she announced calmly, making Sheena's eyes open a shade wider. ' 'sides,' she went on, with a look in her eyes that said that she was thoroughly enjoying herself, 'you're in Grandma's room.'

Sheena was certain that Vicky was now indulging in a daydream at her expense, and began to relax a little. It did no harm to indulge her here. 'I don't see what that's got to do with it,' she answered, giving the little girl a smile that showed that she was well aware of what she was up to.

Vicky gave her a long earnest look, then moved up closer to her. 'You don't believe me, do you?' she replied in a lofty manner. 'Well, I know something you don't know, and I'm not sure that I'm going to tell you,' she added, just as loftily.

Sheena surveyed her with her head on one side and gave her a searching look. 'Perhaps it's better if I don't know,' she answered quietly. 'I'm not sure your uncle would care to have us talking about him in this manner.'

'He wouldn't if it were anybody else,' answered Vicky. 'But you're practically family, so it doesn't matter.'

Sheena frowned back at her. 'Family?' she repeated, beginning to feel a little out of her depth.

Vicky nodded vigorously. 'It's a family secret that we used to share with Clay,' her eyes held a shadow in them at this point. 'When Grandma was here, that was,' she added slowly.

Sheena did not know what to say. She knew that she was on delicate ground and wanted to keep their relationship on an even keel. 'I never knew my grandmother,' she said quietly. 'Mother used to tell me about her when I was young, and I used to wish I had known her. You're lucky that you knew your grandmother, Vicky.'

As soon as she had said this, Sheena almost winced. Her choice of words had not been at all helpful, for in truth of fact Vicky was the most unlucky girl she had met. Only the fact that she was not supposed to know the fate of Vicky's parents saved her from making a swift apology for her thoughtlessness.

To her utter relief Vicky acknowledged her senti-

ments with a little sigh, showing no sign of upset at
her comments. 'Grandma used to hate anyone using
her room—even as a dressing-room when we had
guests—and we used to have lots,' she added wistfully. 'Clay used to tease her about it. He once said
that the only person he would allow to use it would
be the woman he married.' She looked back at
Sheena swiftly to see her reaction to this news.

Sheena's brows lifted, but apart from this there
was no other reaction and Vicky must have been disappointed. 'That was a family joke, Vicky,' she said
lightly. 'You said so yourself. Things are different
now——' She hesitated, not quite knowing how to
state the obvious.

'Now that Grandma's gone, you mean?' Vicky cut
in swiftly, with the light of challenge in her eyes.
'Well, it's not so! It started as a joke, but Clay meant
it! We've had other guests since then, but no one
gets Grandma's room,' she declared vehemently.
'You'll see!' she ended on what sounded remarkably
like a threat, and left Sheena with a nasty suspicion
that mock engagement or no, she would very probably have to marry Clay in the end, if only to prevent
Vicky from losing faith in her uncle!

Once again Sheena was at a loss for words. If she
argued the point, and judging by the light in Vicky's
eyes she was waiting for her to do that, she just might
say something that was better left unsaid. She sighed
inwardly. Vicky's uncle Clay had not left her much
of a loophole should she decide to back out of the
arrangement. Not that that would worry him, she

thought crossly. His only wish was that his niece should be a normal happy child, and he wasn't too bothered about the methods used to gain his goal.

'All right, I'll see,' she temporised with a wry grin, not knowing how else to counteract Vicky's insistence.

Vicky gave a small curt nod, that reminded Sheena of Clay, and that showed that she was well pleased with herself. 'Clay said I was to show you over the place,' she said happily. 'Shall we do it now? We've heaps of time before dinner.'

Sheena, glad that the other subject had been dropped, replied lightly that as long as they were back in time for her to have a shower and change before dinner, she thought it was a good idea.

The homestead was larger than Barter's Ridge, Sheena discovered, even without the added wing to accommodate extra guests. In all there were six bedrooms on the first floor, and two bathrooms. The ground floor contained a large well-furnished lounge and opening off it was an even larger room used as a playroom. At the further end was a full-sized billiards table, and in the middle of the room was a table tennis table.

All ages, it appeared, had been catered for Sheena thought, as her eyes rested on what must have been the children's corner of the large room. A well-used rocking horse badly in need of a coat of paint bore mute witness to this. On top of a battered-looking child's desk lay boxes of games and picture puzzles.

An odd feeling came over Sheena as she took in

all these evidences of a close, happy family. It was a feeling that she had never experienced before. It was as if she belonged there. That this old welcoming homestead had been waiting for her, and was not unfamiliar to her in any way.

Her eyes were misty as she followed Vicky's slight figure out of the playroom and into a roomy study next to it.

'If Clay's in here he doesn't like to be disturbed,' Vicky said, as Sheena gazed around the room. A large desk placed by a window at the end of the room gave the occupant an uninterrupted view of the dairy area and the surrounding paddocks.

The shelves on the wall around the room were packed with books and represented a small library. Sheena's gaze left the books and lingered on several old photographic prints hung above the shelves. That some were sepia-coloured gave an indication of their age, and had Sheena been alone she would have liked to have looked closer at them, as they were obviously family photographs.

'I don't suppose he'd mind if it was you,' Vicky commented thoughtfully, darting Sheena a conspiratorial look that she chose to ignore.

Her confident prediction that whatever she did was sure to be all right with her uncle made Sheena devoutly wish that she could refute this prediction. On recalling Clay's hard features, she was sure that Vicky would soon find that she had overestimated her importance.

On this thought Sheena felt a surge of anger against

Clay for putting her in this position, as she would have not only to watch her words, but always be on the lookout for discrepancies in speech where Vicky was concerned, and it was bound to make their association an extremely tenuous one, quite apart from the fact that she did not relish the role Clay had assigned her to play.

Vicky then led her through another passage and into the dining room, and through an open door the other side of the room through which she could see the lounge, and knew that they had completed the circuit of the ground floor.

The dining room had the same age-old atmosphere as the rest of the homestead, and managed to look homely as well as elegant in spite of the impressive display of silver on a beautifully carved sideboard placed against the wall at the end of the room. The large dark highly polished table in the centre of the room was large enough to seat a dozen people quite comfortably, Sheena noticed.

'I expect Cynthia will be inviting herself over for dinner before long,' Vicky said musingly.

Sheena sensed that she was expected to show an interest in this calm observation but declined the offer, but Vicky was not so easily diverted. 'She thinks Clay will marry her,' she said, with a trace of scorn in her voice, then added in a tone of undisguised pleasure, 'Just wait till she sees you!'

'You're making me feel like some kind of freak!' Sheena said crossly, and glanced meaningly at her watch. 'Isn't it time we got ready for dinner?' she asked, and frowned at Vicky's abrupt chuckle at her accusation.

'Clay won't mind if we're late,' Vicky answered airily. 'Not when he knows I've been showing you over the house.'

'Whether he minds or not,' replied Sheena primly, 'I do mind, and I don't like being late for meals. There's Pietro to consider too, remember?' she added as she walked to the door.

'Oh, Pietro won't mind if Clay doesn't,' answered the incorrigible Vicky. She darted Sheena a look of mischief. 'I suppose you want to pretty up, do you?'

Sheena cast her an exasperated look; she couldn't win! 'If you say so,' she replied dryly, and gave a wry grin as she caught Vicky's knowing nod.

During dinner that evening, which was as good as any special dish of Cookie's, Sheena had to suffer Vicky's undisguised interest in her relations with Clay. She would watch one and then the other, and it was a relief when the meal was over and Clay announced that he had some paper work to catch up on, and could the girls entertain each other?

As Sheena saw Vicky's slight start of surprise at this announcement, she had to hide a swift smile. Vicky was in for a few more surprises if she expected her uncle to down tools and alter his way of life because of her arrival. She was also extremely relieved, since it appeared that whatever he had planned should happen in the future, he did not intend to rush his fences, and this would give her ample time to adjust to the situation.

When they reached the games room, Vicky challenged Sheena to a game of table tennis and was delighted to learn that she could play. 'Cynthia can't,' she said, and again Sheena detected the note of scorn in her voice. 'Thinks any game is a waste of time,' she added, as she handed Sheena a bat and gave her the ball, indicating that she should serve first.

Sheena said nothing, but stationed herself at the end of the table and started serving. The game brought back painful memories of Doyle, since it was Doyle who had taught her to play at the start of their courtship.

Vicky was no mean player herself, and after four games the honours were even, and it was decided that they should play one more game to find the winner.

'Clay taught me to play,' commented Vicky, as they began the final game. 'Who taught you?'

Sheena looked down at her bat, giving herself time to think before she answered as airily as she could manage. 'Oh, a friend of mine,' and hoped that would be that.

'Boy-friend?' queried the astute Vicky.

'As a matter-of-fact, yes,' replied Sheena, giving studious attention to her service station.

'And you're missing him?' prodded Vicky, with a flash of feminine intuition.

Sheena lifted her bat in return to a high ball of Vicky's and attempted to give the ball a winning smash to her side of the table, but she missed the edge of the table completely and lost the point. 'I suppose

I am,' she replied, tight-lipped. It was the truth and she didn't particularly care who knew it at that point in time.

'Then you shouldn't have let Clay bring you here,' answered Vicky solemnly. 'If he wants to marry you, then you'd better forget that other boy-friend,' she added significantly.

Sheena slapped her bat down on the table and gave the little girl an exasperated look. 'It's not like that at all,' she said sternly. 'My father wanted me to come here, so there was a good reason why I came, and why I shall probably stay, but I don't have to. If I want to go down South again, then I shall do just that. I'm very grateful for your uncle's help, but as I told you, I haven't anywhere to stay until my father's place is rebuilt.'

'That old place on the edge of the property?' said Vicky with raised brows. 'You can't stay there!' she exclaimed indignantly. 'Clay won't let you,' she added adamantly.

'It's not up to Clay,' replied Sheena, with as much dignity as she could muster, although she wanted to shout the words. 'My father left me the smallholding, and I intend to carry on where he left off.'

'Not if Clay says otherwise,' interrupted Vicky firmly, making Sheena take a deep breath and pray for patience in dealing with this altogether too assured child.

'Not if Clay says otherwise about what?' queried a dulcet voice behind them, and both of them turned to face the woman who stood just inside the door. 'Well?' she went on, in a low seductive drawl as she crossed the room towards them. 'I'm intrigued. Who's been upsetting Clay?'

'No one's been upsetting Clay,' replied Vicky, a frown of displeasure showing her feelings at this interruption. 'It's just that Sheena wants to work on that old smallholding that he let Mr Greig have, and I don't think he'll let her,' she answered abruptly, as if hating to impart even this news to the immaculately turned out brunette now giving Sheena a long calculating look out of her large dark eyes, the size of which was emphasized by a line of mascara around the lids.

'And you are?' she asked, with a note of patronage in her voice that was not lost on Sheena, who had not liked the way the woman had scrutinised her.

'She's Clay's girl-friend,' answered Vicky quickly, with a gleam of appreciation in her eyes at the woman's obvious astonishment at this statement. 'Clay brought her back with him from Sydney,' she supplied helpfully, then added as an afterthought, 'This is Cynthia Layton, Sheena.'

Sheena gave the naughty Vicky a frown of displeasure before she held out her hand to Cynthia. 'Sheena Greig,' she said, finishing Vicky's nonchalant introduction. 'The smallholding belonged to my father, and don't take any notice of what Vicky's just said, she's having you on.'

'I'm not so!' Vicky replied indignantly. 'Tell her what room you've been given,' she commanded Sheena, then without giving her time to answer, she went on, 'She's got Gran's room!'

'I don't see that that means anything,' replied

Sheena, feeling an urge to slap Vicky.

'Well, it wouldn't, would it?' answered Vicky, before Sheena could go on. 'I told you that, didn't I? But it does to us, doesn't it, Cynthia?' she appealed, darting a malicious glance at the woman whose large dark eyes had now narrowed in speculation as they rested on the uncomfortable Sheena.

'I agree with Miss Greig, and wouldn't put any meaning on that,' she answered stiffly, and Sheena felt she was being given a 'keep off the grass' warning where Clay was concerned. 'It's the room next to yours, isn't it?' she asked Vicky. 'I expect that's why she was given it. Being a stranger, she wouldn't feel quite so isolated as she would be if she had one of the guest rooms further along the corridor.'

Sheena did not miss the emphasised 'stranger', but it did not bother her—she was a stranger, and had no intention of encroaching on her territory although this lovely but hard-looking woman would find that hard to believe. Clay's suggestion that they should enter into a mock engagement appeared even more ludicrous than it had at first to her, and she wondered if Miss Layton would be put into the picture at some later stage of the plot. She devoutly hoped so, since she could almost feel the waves of hostility emanating from her.

'He gave you one of the guest rooms when you stayed here last month,' Vicky shot out at her triumphantly.

'But I'm not a stranger, am I, dear?' replied Cynthia sweetly, giving Vicky a look that told Sheena that she wasn't the only one who would like to slap Vicky.

'You're not his bride-to-be, either!' Vicky snapped back at her.

'Vicky!' gasped Sheena, feeling that things had gone far enough.

'I prefer to forget that remark, Vicky,' said Cynthia, out of narrow lips. 'I keep forgetting that you're not well,' she added spitefully, and although Sheena could well understand her chagrin, she could not condone that.

'I'm not an idiot either!' Vicky flung back at her furiously. 'I'm right this time—just you wait and see!'

'Is this a private fight, or a free-for-all?' Clay enquired in an amused voice, as he entered the room. His dark glance rested briefly on Sheena, who looked as embarrassed as she felt, and then went from the bright-cheeked Vicky to the pursed-up lips of Cynthia, and back to Sheena again. 'Don't worry, Sheena,' he said airily, 'these two enjoy sparring with each other. You'll get used to it. I wouldn't advise you to take sides, though, they're quite capable of fending for themselves.'

'Clay!' gasped Cynthia, and flung a look of pure venom towards the smirking Vicky who had achieved a remarkable victory over her enemy by having her classed in the same category as herself, even though there must have been ten years' difference in their ages. 'If you knew what we were discussing, you'd take my side this time. Ask Vicky about it later, and

tell her she can apologise the next time we meet,'
then she added meaningly, 'I think it's time she went
to bed.'

'I'll go to bed when I want to!' Vicky almost spat
out at her. 'And it's nothing to do with you when I
go!'

'Vicky!' said Clay, on a warning note. 'This time
Cynthia's right, and you know it. Off you go, you can
finish your fight some other time.'

It was Cynthia this time who received a venomous
look from Vicky. 'Very well,' she said, with as much
dignity as she could muster, 'but I don't mind telling
Clay what we were talking about,' she announced
airily, as she walked to the door. 'Goodnight,
Sheena,' she said politely, and gave Clay a conspiratorial look, but completely ignored Cynthia, and left
the room.

Clay's expressive eyebrows rose as he looked back
at Sheena and Cynthia, and Sheena cowardly decided to follow Vicky's exit and made a move towards the door, but was forestalled by Clay's, 'It's
not that bad, is it?'

'Of course not!' Sheena replied quickly, too
quickly, and received a searching look from Clay. 'I
think Vicky enjoys riling people, and I'm sure Miss
Layton knows her well enough to understand that,
and not take her teasing too seriously.'

'Considering the subject, I could hardly pass it
over,' retorted Cynthia, in a voice meant to convey
her wounded feelings over what was said.

Her answer had the desired effect on Clay, who

walked over to a reclining chair opposite to the one Cynthia occupied, and nodded towards another chair beside it. 'Sit down, Sheena,' he said casually. 'I want to know just what that impish niece of mine is up to now,' and when Sheena hesitated, and was about to plead tiredness, he forestalled her again with, 'Don't tell me you're tired, you slept most of the way in the car coming up here, remember?'

Sheena's cheeks flamed, and to hide her embarrassment she did exactly what she didn't want to do and sat down in the chair he held out for her. There was something in the way that he had said that that made it sound much more than just falling asleep on a long journey, and by the way Cynthia was looking at her there was no doubt that her thoughts were running on the same lines.

'Well?' asked Clay, in the tiny silence that followed.

'She was on about Miss Greig having been given your mother's room,' Cynthia said quickly, as if trying to dispel certain unwelcome thoughts that had entered her mind after Clay's remarks about their journey from Sydney. 'She seems to have got the ridiculous idea that you're carrying on with that old promise of yours to your mother. You'd better watch out, Clay, she'll have you married off to poor Miss Greig before you know it.' She gave him a sweet sympathetic smile. 'You know how she gets these fixations, but this is obviously one that ought to be nipped in the bud, and the sooner the better.'

Clay gave a wicked grin and looked at the cringing Sheena, who wished that she could somehow become invisible. 'Are you "poor Miss Greig"?' he asked her with a teasing quality in his voice.

'Right now, that's precisely how I would describe myself!' retorted Sheena angrily, feeling that she was being made fun of and that it was about time that she made her feelings quite clear about this. She was getting tired of being on the receiving end of Clay and Vicky's new source of amusement.

Her heated reply obviously pleased Cynthia, who went as far as to actually smile at her. 'Don't worry, Miss Greig,' she said sympathetically. 'No one takes Vicky seriously—inside the family, that is—and as long as Clay knows what she's up to, there'll be no harm done.'

'Ever thought that Vicky could be right?' queried Clay casually, looking directly at Cynthia, who visibly blanched and stared back at him with wide eyes.

'Clay!' she exclaimed, on a note of censure after the shock had partially worn off. 'You're as bad as Vicky! For goodness' sake, what must Miss Greig think? She'll wonder if she's landed in some kind of madhouse!'

Miss Greig was incapable of thinking anything at that precise time, except that Clay had decided to go ahead with the mock engagement with her. It was also clear that he did not intend to put Cynthia Layton into the picture. Considering her private war with his niece, this was not altogether surprising, but Sheena would have liked more notice of his intentions, and felt that she had been thrown into an arena and left to survive as best she could.

Sheena looked from the tight-lipped Cynthia, who moved restlessly in her chair and crossed one elegantly hosed leg over the other, exposing a length of leg casually as if by accident, but it was a well-practised action and made Sheena wonder if she was a model too, as Vicky's mother had been. She had the looks as well as the figure, and her clothes were expensive and worn with a casual elegance. Her gaze left Cynthia and rested on Clay, and she was annoyed to find that he was studying her and seemed to be waiting for some comment from her. What was she supposed to say? she wondered crossly. Perhaps Cynthia had been right and she had landed in a madhouse!

It was the thought of her survival that made her say stiffly, 'I suppose no one minds if I comment on the fact that Vicky appears to have taken after her uncle, and has the same sense of humour.' Her eyes shone blue fire as they clashed with Clay's black enigmatical ones. She knew she was going back on her word, but he had forced the issue without giving her a fair chance of acting the part. She felt no remorse, he had only himself to blame.

Clay's eyes held hers, and Sheena felt their magnetic hold on her and wanted to look away, but couldn't. It was Clay who broke what seemed to be some kind of spell on her by turning his dark gaze on Cynthia. 'What do you say to that, Cynthia? Would you say I was some kind of joker?'

Cynthia tried to give a casual shrug, but it turned

into a helpless bewildered movement, and Sheena hated Clay for his insensitivity towards this woman who was obviously in love with him. 'I wouldn't have said so,' she replied in a low voice, 'but I'm not so sure now.' She stared at Sheena. 'You've not wasted much time, have you?' she flung out at her. 'I've known some quick workers in my time, but you must hold the record!' she spat out at Sheena, badly wanting a whipping boy to vent her frustration on.

'Hold your fire, Cynthia,' Clay said softly but warningly. 'You ought to know better than that. Since when have I been influenced by a pretty face? I make my own decisions, as you well know.' His dark gaze rested on Sheena. 'And you've got it all wrong. Sheena's not chasing me, her affections lie elsewhere, but I intend to change all that, so perhaps it is poor Miss Greig, wouldn't you agree?' he asked with deceptive casualness.

Sheena stood up quickly—enough was enough! 'I'm sure you can finish this intriguing discussion without me,' she ground out furiously. 'I hope I've provided you both with good entertainment for the evening. Don't bother to have that place rebuilt, Mr Dayman,' she spat out at him as she walked to the door, 'I've decided not to stay.'

Her fury mounted as she heard Clay give a low chuckle, 'Goodnight, Sheena, you'll feel different tomorrow.'

CHAPTER SEVEN

As Sheena passed Vicky's room she was relieved to see that her door was closed. She had half expected to find her waiting up for her, and she had had quite enough of the remarkable Dayman family for one day.

When she reached her room she lost no time in taking a shower, and thankfully shutting her bedroom door firmly behind her, got swiftly into bed. Woe betide Vicky if she made an entrance now, she thought darkly, for Sheena's sympathy lay entirely with Cynthia Layton. She might not like the woman, but it was patently obvious that she had had a rough deal from Clay, not to mention Vicky's blatant hostility and goading insolence, not at all in keeping with her age.

Sheena bunched her pillows up under her head, and thinking that she heard a footstep outside her bedroom door, quickly switched out her bedside light. If it was Vicky, she would feign sleep, she told herself, but as the seconds passed and the door remained closed, she was able to relax and give her attention to the unenviable position she had landed herself in.

The grand statement that she would be leaving weighed heavily on her mind. Where could she go?

And where would she get a job? She had no money
—at least, not yet—and whatever her father had left
her, she would have to wait for Clay to see to that
side of affairs for her.

She turned restlessly. In other words she was in a
cleft stick, and Clay Dayman knew it. No wonder he
had sounded so sure of himself when he had said that
she would feel different tomorrow! What a fool she
had been in blindly accepting his offer to bring her
north with him. But she hadn't accepted, she reminded herself bleakly, recalling the way he had
simply taken over her life.

Even if she had changed her mind—and if Doyle
had managed to talk her out of it—she knew with an
odd certainty that Clay wouldn't have left it at that.
It wouldn't have made any difference if Doyle hadn't
lost control and tried to force her to stay the only way
he knew how to. Nothing short of a wedding ring on
her finger would have stopped Clay Dayman from
carrying out her father's wishes. Sheena knew this as
well as she knew she didn't like Clay Dayman—or
his single-minded way of going about things.

Her eyes closed as she relived her last night at
Barter's Ridge, and once again felt Doyle's lips caress-
ing her. Only the timely intervention of Mrs Charter
had prevented her self-betrayal and the inevitable result.

She knew she ought to be grateful that fate had
watched over her, but she didn't feel particularly
grateful right then. She felt bereft, and cheated out
of the fulfilment of her dreams. So Doyle was proud,

and weak where she was concerned—well, she didn't blame him for that. Who was she anyway? Just a little nobody who happened to be his manager's daughter, and whom he would have married had her father not betrayed his trust.

She then thought of Cynthia Layton who loved Clay, but Clay didn't love her, and no amount of wishful thinking would change things for her. In a way she had much in common with the luckless Cynthia. She loved Doyle, and although he had wanted her, he had not loved her enough to marry her.

Clay's assertive claim that he intended to push the memory of Doyle out of her life, whether this had been said to lay the foundation of their mock engagement or not, was a non-starter as far as Sheena was concerned. She had loved Doyle too long to even hope that she could forget him, even while bitterly conceding that she stood no chance of happiness until she did.

She fell asleep on the bleak thought that she would have to stay at Rimini for a few more days at least, and somehow fend off Vicky's assured predictions of her uncle's intentions where she was concerned. There would also be an unhappy Cynthia to contend with, since Sheena could not see her bowing out of the picture; she was not the type to give up that easily. Between her and the incorrigible Vicky, not to mention the bulldozing tactics of her formidable uncle, she could see anything but a peaceful existence ahead of her.

Until breakfast the following morning, Sheena was

left in peace, and it did occur to her that perhaps Clay had given Vicky an order to stay away from her, correctly assuming that Sheena would be in no mood for another dose of Vicky's enlightened comments on her future.

When Sheena arrived in the kitchen for breakfast, she found Vicky on the point of finishing her meal, and devoutly hoped that she would take herself off to whatever pursuit she had in mind for that morning without seeking her company. Her hopes, however, were doomed to disappointment as Vicky made no move to leave the table after her breakfast. 'Clay doesn't take breakfast,' she said, seeing Sheena glance at the empty seat occupied by Clay the previous day.

Sheena gave a nod at this unasked-for information, but she was relieved to be spared his autocratic company at the start of the day.

'That reminds me,' went on Vicky, 'he wants you to take him his morning coffee at ten-thirty. He's working in the study,' she offered helpfully.

Sheena seated herself at the breakfast table, and on Pietro's swift appearance with her breakfast, she thanked him, and wondered absently how she would be able to do justice to the generous portion of eggs and bacon that he had served her with. 'Who usually takes his morning coffee in?' she queried lightly, yet with a touch of annoyance in her voice that Vicky did not miss.

'Usually Pietro, but I do if he's extra busy,' Vicky replied carefully.

'I wouldn't want to step on anyone's toes,' Sheena replied, with a touch of sarcasm in her voice.

'I suppose he wants to talk to you,' answered Vicky, with an innocent look that belied the knowing look in her eyes.

'Very likely!' Sheena said dryly, as she settled to her meal. She wanted to talk to Clay too. There were a few things she wanted to get straight before she let herself in for any more evenings like the last one. Shock tactics weren't in it!

'We've a tennis court at the back of the house,' Vicky said quickly, wisely changing the conversation. 'Do you play?' she asked hopefully.

Sheena chewed and swallowed a crisp piece of bacon before she answered, surprised how hungry she had been and having no trouble in clearing her plate. 'I've had one or two games, but I can't say I'm any good at it.'

'Doesn't matter,' Vicky said quickly. 'I can teach you if you'd like a game—besides,' she added airily, 'that way we can keep out of Cynthia's way if she decides to call in—and I'll bet she does,' she ended darkly.

Sheena poured herself a cup of coffee, and took her time in replying. 'Why do you dislike her so much, Vicky?' she asked her slowly.

Vicky shrugged impatiently. 'It's not only me,' she said defensively. 'No one likes her. We only put up with her because Clay——' she didn't finish the rest of the sentence, but Sheena knew what she meant. Clay had encouraged Cynthia to hang around, but was now tired of her. On recalling what had been said the previous evening, Sheena realised he was making it quite clear that whatever attraction Cynthia had once held for him, it was now over. She felt a spurt of pity for her, and a surge of anger against Clay Dayman. It was so easy for a man.

'Mum doesn't like her, either,' Vicky added, with a glint of defiance in her eye as she looked straight at Sheena, and Sheena wondered how to tackle this latest move of hers on this delicate subject. She had clearly said 'doesn't' and not 'didn't', and that meant that she was determined to carry on with her pathetic makebelieve.

'She's a model, isn't she?' queried Sheena, deciding to take the coward's way out and not force the issue.

Vicky gave another disdainful shrug. 'She'll never make the top, like Mum,' she said on a disparaging note. 'You've either got it or you haven't. She looks all right, and she's got the figure, but you have to have more than that,' she told Sheena earnestly. 'I've some photographs of Mum,' she added, as she got up hastily from her chair, 'you'll see what I mean then when I show you them,' and rushed out of the kitchen.

Sheena finished her coffee and stared at the bright tiles of the kitchen. She felt immensely sad, and knew she would feel even sadder as she looked at the photographs that Vicky was going to show her. Pictures of a lovely woman who had died so tragically at the height of her career—and not only her, but Vicky's father, too.

Her blue eyes that spoke her feelings so clearly met Pietro's sympathetic brown ones as he cleared the breakfast table, and without realising it she spoke her thoughts aloud. 'What does one do?' she asked in a low despondent voice.

Pietro's thin wiry figure straightened as he lifted the tray of used crockery, and he smiled at Sheena. 'What we all do,' he said, with a trace of an accent in his voice. 'Try and make it easy for her.' He gave an expressive shrug. 'She's young yet. I think maybe all will be right,' and he left Sheena to her musings.

It was even harder than Sheena had thought it would be. As she gazed at the photographs in the thick album that Vicky had brought back with her, she was lost for words. Her mother was all that Vicky had claimed, and Sheena, staring at the image of the lovely woman posing in a clinging velvet dress on the front of an expensive glossy magazine, was able to understand what Vicky had meant when she had said that there was more to modelling than having looks and a good figure.

Whatever the secret was, there was no denying that this beautiful woman had possessed it. There was an ethereal quality about her, and the large dark lovely eyes that stared back at you from the glossy cover seemed to be challenging you to find fault with such matchless beauty. The eyes particularly reminded Sheena of Clay. They had the same mesmeric gaze, only his was compelling and hers was guileless.

That such a lovely creature should perish was a tragedy, but even more tragic was the thought that the tall good-looking man by her side, shown in a later picture, and proudly pointed out by Vicky as her father, should have shared the same fate.

The only comforting thought was that they had gone together, but Vicky had been left to pick up the pieces. No wonder she had closed her mind on the doors of grief, refusing to acknowledge that such a thing could happen. Sheena looked at her dark curly head as she bent over the album lovingly fingering the pages as each one was turned, and was almost persuaded that the child should be left to her dreams, for that was all that she had left.

She shook her head bewilderedly. It was no use thinking like that. Somehow Vicky had to be helped to come to terms with the blow fate had dealt her and the sooner the better. Her heart was heavy as she followed Vicky out of the kitchen a short while later and through to the sectioned-off part of lawn used as a tennis court. For the life of her she couldn't see how to bring about the desired result. It was just as Pietro had said. They could only hope for the best and try and make things easy for her.

The hour the girls spent on the tennis court proved a relaxing occupation for both of them. Sheena found herself hoping that they could carry on playing, and that Pietro would take in Clay's coffee. She wanted to postpone their meeting for as long as possible, particularly after what had been said the previous evening. The way she felt about things there were bound to be a few home truths aired, and she didn't feel ready or brave enough to enter into battle with such a forbidding character as Clay Dayman, who had a nasty habit of coming out on top at every confrontation she had had with him.

Her hopes of a reprieve were dashed by Vicky's unhelpful, 'Golly, it's almost half past! You'd better get back to the kitchen, Sheena. Pietro will have Clay's coffee ready.'

With such a reminder, Sheena could hardly argue the point, and with lagging footsteps she followed Vicky back to the homestead.

As predicted by Vicky, Pietro had set aside a tray containing a pot of coffee, and ominously, from Sheena's point of view, two cups and saucers. Vicky's knowing nod, and casual 'I'll see you later, Sheena,' did nothing to soothe Sheena's apprehension at the coming meeting with Clay.

Sheena's hands were not quite steady as she carried the tray from the kitchen to the study. When she knocked on the study door and Clay's deep voice bade her enter, she heard another voice in the background as she obeyed the summons. A wild hope that he might have company surged through her, only to be quashed dismally as she saw that he was using a dictating machine and was playing back a section of tape.

At her entry he switched off the machine and gave her a forbidding look that left her in no doubt that he was displeased with her, and nodded curtly towards an empty space on his desk indicating that

that was where she should put the tray.

Her hands were even more unsteady as she placed the tray down, but her lips were tightly pressed together. If he wanted a fight he could have one, she told herself. Anyone would think he was the injured party, she thought indignantly, and what a nerve he had! Expecting her to toe the line after what had happened the previous evening! If only she could just walk out—if only she had somewhere to go—whispered her heart desolately.

She half expected him to demand that she pour their coffee out, but to her slight surprise he did not, but tackled the task himself, glancing up at her under his dark brows as he did so. 'You can sit down,' he said autocratically. 'You're not going anywhere.'

Sheena selected a chair as far away from the desk as possible, and collecting the coffee that he held out for her, settled herself down. Her thoughts were far from serene. There had been a certain inflection in his voice that she hadn't cared for at all, a kind of warning to her to toe the line or else, and a slight shiver went through her.

Her smouldering blue eyes surveyed the dark features of Clay Dayman as she sipped her coffee slowly. She wasn't going to be browbeaten by this man. What did she know of him anyway? So he had been kind to her father—well, she had tried to repay him for that—and might still have carried out his wishes if he hadn't adopted such bulldozing tactics. That she was being used as a pawn was not a comfortable thought, not even when it was for a good cause, but she had been willing to accept such a role for Vicky's sake. Now she wasn't too sure that this autocratic male wasn't using her for quite another purpose.

A purpose that wasn't too hard to spot—it was, in fact, crystal clear from where Sheena sat—he was tired of Cynthia and was using Sheena to clear the decks for him. Only Sheena was not going to play that particular game with him. That was entirely his business and nothing to do with her and if she got the chance she would tell him so, she thought furiously.

'I hope you've had time to reconsider your rather hasty remarks about leaving,' Clay said, in a forbidding tone. 'You did agree to stay and see things through, for Vicky's sake if nothing else,' he added coldly, making Sheena feel that she had let him down at the worst possible time.

'And I meant to do just that,' she replied, just as coldly, showing him that she was not going to let him walk all over her. 'Before last night, that was,' she went on swiftly, her anger now mounting. 'But I didn't expect to be thrown into the fray quite so early after my arrival. You might have warned me,' she accused him tartly.

'Of what?' he enquired, with a lift of his autocratic brows.

Sheena took a deep breath. Not for anything would she allow him to see that the question had thrown her, since the answer should have been obvious to anyone else but this man who made his own rules and expected her to comply with them. 'I'm referring to Miss Layton,' she said through stiff lips, her blue eyes sending off warning sparks to him not to dodge the issue.

Her heart quailed at the answering flash of fury in his dark eyes, but she was determined to hold her ground. If it was his private business, he shouldn't have brought her into it, she told herself stoutly.

'I fail to see what Cynthia has to do with our private arrangement,' he said haughtily. 'Or just what you're worried about.' He gave Sheena a long considering look. 'I don't intend to make passionate love to you—in case that's what's worrying you.'

A bright flush stained Sheena's cheeks and her coffee cup rattled in the saucer so loudly that she had to put it down quickly to avoid spilling coffee all over the carpet.

'So it is that,' said Clay, with a trace of amusement in his dark eyes. 'Well, I promise not to step out of line.' His eyes travelled lightly yet somehow speculatively over her embarrassed features. 'I seem to recall giving you the same assurance earlier,' he added lightly. 'So I'm repeating it. You have no cause whatsoever to back out on those premises.'

Sheena could have hit him. He had cleverly dodged the issue and left her floundering in a sea of indecision. Whatever his intentions were regarding Cynthia Layton, it was no business of hers, and she felt that he was telling her this in no uncertain way. She also felt gauche and unwanted. She had felt bad enough after her flight from Barter's Ridge. Doyle had wanted her but had not loved her enough to marry her, and here was this ruthless character underlining her aching sense of failure.

It was as if the very idea of his becoming embroiled with her in any way other than the proposed ploy to cure Vicky was causing him a vast amount of amusement, and it hurt. It hurt more than she would have thought possible. It was more than her pride, and Sheena was bewildered by her feelings. She didn't like this dark hard-faced man, so why should she allow him to get under her skin? In a way he was right, she conceded grudgingly; what right had she to set herself up as judge and jury where his personal relationships were concerned? No right at all, she thought miserably, only she knew what it felt like to be thrown aside. Cynthia was better off without him, as she was better off without Doyle. Better to cut loose and be done with it.

'So we go ahead,' said Clay, in a voice that brooked no refusal. 'You've nothing to lose, and we've both plenty to gain if we reach our objective.'

Sheena remained staring at the rich pattern of the carpet at her feet. She knew she wasn't expected to put up any more resistance. He knew what he wanted, and her personal feelings in the matter did not concern him—never would, she thought bitterly. As for both of them having something to gain—well, she couldn't see what she would get out of the mock engagement. She took a deep breath. There was Vicky, of course, and it was for Vicky's sake that she had agreed to fall in with Clay's preposterous suggestion in the first place.

Sheena swallowed. Once again he had taken the

initiative and made her feel selfish and unfeeling, and it wasn't like that at all, and it was so unfair! It wouldn't be so bad if she hadn't got this certainty that there was more behind the mock engagement ploy than just a sincere wish to cure his niece.

Whatever it was, she was never likely to find out, she told herself. It was then that she recalled what Clay had said earlier about useful side effects. So that was what he had meant by both of them gaining something from the situation. Her slim fingers clenched into a small fist. The man was despicable! He was stamping on her bruised heart just to gain his objective.

She stood up quickly as if unable to bear being in the same room with him. 'Very well,' she said, in a small tight voice. Her eyes said more than words as they clashed with his dark enigmatic ones. 'I gather you've no objection to my broadcasting the news to certain interested parties?' she asked, with a sardonic twist to her voice.

She did not name Doyle. She didn't have to, the sudden narrowing of Clay's eyes told her that he had got the connection. 'I'm taking your advice, you see,' she said quickly. 'You did suggest such a possibility, didn't you?' she added cuttingly.

'So I did,' Clay replied softly. 'I also said something else—something that it might pay you to remember some time.'

Sheena stared back at him. What did he mean by that? A slight frown creased her smooth forehead, but after a moment's thought without enlightenment she shrugged the remark off as just another annoying comment of his to gain the initiative again.

Because his dark eyes were boring into hers, Sheena looked away quickly and bent down to retrieve her cup and saucer, glad of something to do to break the sudden tension between them. 'Shall I take the tray back to the kitchen? Have you finished?' she tacked on quickly, feeling an urgent wish to change the conversation.

'For now, yes,' he answered slowly, then nodded at the tray at his desk. 'Yes, you can take that with you.'

Sheena's hands were even more unsteady when she picked the tray up than when she had first placed it on the desk. When she had asked if he had finished, she had been referring to the coffee and he must have known that, she thought furiously, but he had chosen to place his own interpretation on the mundane remark and answer it with some kind of warning that left her vaguely uneasy, though she couldn't think why.

With relief that their talk was now over, and that was all it could be called, and not a confrontation, Sheena walked to the door. 'By the way, I'm giving a dinner dance tomorrow evening,' Clay announced, as she reached the door, and as Sheena's startled eyes flew to his now mocking ones, he added softly, 'So now I'm warning you, I shall expect a little more cooperation from you from now on.'

The cups fairly rattled in the tray that Sheena held and she had to grip the tray hard to hold it steady after this startling announcement. The fact that he was amused by her reaction turned her apprehension into fury and she managed to reply on an icy note, 'I shall do my best,' and only just managed to refrain from banging the door hard after her.

CHAPTER EIGHT

SHEENA'S ruffled composure was somewhat soothed by the sympathetic Vicky, who after taking one look at the storm signs in Sheena's eyes when she arrived back in the kitchen with the coffee tray, tactfully suggested that they play a game of table tennis.

Had Sheena been given a choice as to how she filled in the rest of the morning until lunch, she would have preferred to be on her own. Her encounter with Clay had left her in a very bemused state. There had been a certain inflection in his voice when referring to future events, such as the dinner dance he was giving the following evening.

She had felt gauche and unsure of herself before, but now she was even more so. On the face of things she had nothing to worry about, yet she was worried and wished she could define the cause of her unrest.

Clay had used her attachment to Doyle as a cover for her disinterest in him where the romantic stakes were concerned purely to convince Cynthia of his intentions, but Sheena had a nasty feeling that it was a tactic that he would continue to use whenever the occasion offered itself. Particularly if she failed to come up to scratch. On this thought her firm lips clamped together as they entered the games room, and she selected a bat and stood ready to receive the first service from Vicky.

It was really extremely clever of him, she thought as she settled down to the game. By promoting the suggestion that his pursuance of her affections was an uphill task, he would leave himself completely free from any outward display of affection towards her— physically so, that was—and there would only be his spoken endearments to contend with whenever they were in company.

On reflection of this point, Sheena knew that she ought to be extremely grateful for his thoughtfulness on her behalf, but she couldn't rid herself of the suspicion that he had a double purpose in mind. She had thought it had been part and parcel of the removal of Cynthia from the scene, but now she was having second thoughts on that, and that brought her mind back to the dinner party.

'Clay's giving a dinner dance tomorrow night,' she said casually to Vicky as she retrieved the ball from the floor where a smash of Vicky's had scored a point for her. 'Did you know?' she asked her, as she threw the ball over to her.

Vicky paused a moment before she got on with the game. 'No,' she replied. 'He didn't say anything to me, but then he doesn't. I'm not supposed to be present at those kind of do's, but I usually sneak down and raid some eats before they've all gone.' She grinned at Sheena. 'It's no use waiting to the next day in the hope of left-overs. Pietro's pastries are famous around here. Besides,' she added simply, 'I like to see the dresses. I get a good view from the top of the stairs—they can't see me, but I can see them.'

On the mention of dresses, Sheena quickly changed the subject, fearing another lapse of Vicky's into her dream world. 'It's rather quick notice, isn't it?' she queried lightly. 'I mean, surely a dinner dance takes a while to organise? Has he got a band on tap, or something?'

Vicky's dark brows so like her uncle's, lifted at this. 'Oh, it's not a big affair,' she replied, 'although the women dress up for it, particularly a few I could mention,' she added darkly, thinking, Sheena surmised, of Cynthia Layton. 'There won't be more than eight guests, and they'll all be neighbours,' she went on. 'It's a sort of get-together, really. As for a band, we don't need one.' She nodded towards a cabinet at the end of the room. 'We've a hi-fi, and plenty of good records. I can't dance, can you?' she suddenly asked Sheena.

Sheena, whose thoughts had been on the neighbourly get-together and who was already beginning to feel a few qualms at the thought, blinked as she considered the question. Doyle had taught her to dance, and as with other painful memories it was something she would prefer not to dwell on, so she hastily replied in the affirmative and smashed back a winning return to Vicky that gave her the game, and would, she hoped, turn her thoughts in another direction.

Sheena might have known that her tactics wouldn't work, but at least Vicky's next question

was not the embarrassing one she had feared, such as
who had taught her to dance.

'What will you wear?' she asked Sheena.

Sheena stared at her. What would she wear? She
had nothing in the evening dress line. She had had no
occasion to buy one, even if she could have afforded
one. The dances she had attended with Doyle had
been local affairs and all of them at Barter's Ridge.
'Do they all wear evening dress?' she asked Vicky in
a doubtful voice, not sure if Vicky had been em-
broidering a little on this.

Vicky nodded her head firmly. 'The men just wear
dark suits,' she replied. 'But the women go to town.
You'll see. Haven't you got an evening dress?' she
asked curiously.

Sheena shook her head. 'I don't come from those
sort of circles,' she answered simply. 'We had dances,
but not the sort you dress up for.' As she said this an
idea occurred to her that suddenly brightened her
outlook. 'I think I'll sit at the top of the stairs with
you, and we'll share the eats,' she stated, with a
twinkle in her eyes.

'As if Clay would let you!' Vicky said indignantly.
'You're the reason he's giving the party, I bet. We
haven't had one for ages,' she added wistfully.

At the look of sorrow in Vicky's eyes Sheena said
quickly, 'Well, I'll just have to turn up like the
country cousin, won't I? I don't think it will really
matter much, do you?' she added cheerfully.

'Clay won't like that,' said Vicky firmly. 'I'll find
you a dress. There's plenty to choose from——' she

hesitated for a second before she added, 'Mummy's will be too long for you, but Maria's should fit you,' with a gleam of determination in her eyes.

Sheena had been about to expound on the 'Clay won't like it' theme and positively state her views on the matter, but the introduction of another female's name slightly threw her. 'Maria?' she queried.

'Clay's sister—my aunt,' replied Vicky impatiently, in the tone of voice that said that Sheena ought to have known that. 'Come on, let's see what we can find,' she said eagerly, throwing her bat down on to the table with a clutter and making for the door.

On reaching the door and finding that Sheena still stood where she was by the table, she dashed back and grabbed her arm, pulling her towards the door. 'I don't think——' began Sheena, who now found herself being determinedly pulled up the stairs towards a room on the right of the passage, 'that I can possibly wear one of your aunt's dresses.'

'Why not?' asked Vicky, in a surprised voice as she opened the door of the bedroom she was heading for. 'Maria won't mind. She's got heaps of dresses, she and Carlotta were the same size and they often swapped dresses. Carlotta's not so slim now. I suppose having children had something to do with that,' she added thoughtfully, as she opened the doors of a large wardrobe that took up two thirds of the opposite wall. 'You'll have to wear an evening dress, you'll feel awful in an ordinary dress,' she commented absently, as she searched for what she wanted.

'I shall feel worse wearing someone else's dress,'

answered Sheena, just as stubbornly. 'Especially as I haven't got permission to borrow it!'

'Well, think about Clay, then,' Vicky retorted smartly, and gave a grunt of satisfaction as she located the dresses and took them out of the wardrobe. 'There's three here,' she said happily. 'You can try them on, I'm sure they'll fit you.'

'I'll do no such thing!' Sheena replied adamantly, as she watched Vicky lay the dresses out on the bed for her perusal, then at the look of hurt she saw in Vicky's eyes, she added lamely, 'They're very nice.'

As soon as she had said this, Sheena felt what an understatement that had been, for the dresses were quite beautiful and no doubt expensive ones. She didn't want to wear any of them; they were lovely, but they were not for her. To please Vicky, though, she did look at them. There was a pale blue dress of a silken texture with a rather low-looking V-neck, and although Sheena knew the colour would highlight her eyes, the front was much too low for comfort. The second dress was a heavenly wine colour, that would also suit her dark colouring, and would also emphasize the figure, as it was made of a kind of stretch material that would cling close. It was a sophisticated dress, Sheena concluded, and needed to be worn by a sophisticated woman, and certainly not for her.

The third dress was more to her liking. It was white and absolutely plain with a cross-over pleated front, reminiscent of the classical line. The full pleated skirt fell straight from the waist. It was a simple dress, yet an elegant one. Had Sheena had to make a choice, that was the dress she would have chosen, but as she had no intention of borrowing such finery with or without the owner's permission, the question of choice did not arise.

During her quick appraisal of the dresses, Vicky had watched her closely; now she demanded, 'Well? You liked the white one, didn't you? Are you going to try it on?'

Sheena sighed inwardly. When it came to harassment, there wasn't much to choose between Vicky and her uncle! 'No, Vicky, I'm not,' she answered firmly, resolutely looking away from the disappointment shown by Vicky on this firm stand. She had to draw the line somewhere and so far she had not had much success with her uncle, and she did not intend to receive the same treatment from his niece.

'We'll ask Clay about it,' Vicky answered stubbornly.

'Don't you dare!' Sheena replied swiftly. 'If it's the informal affair you said it would be, then it won't matter what I wear. I've got some dresses, and if they're not good enough, then it's just too bad,' she declared fervently, then glanced at her watch. 'It's almost lunch time,' she added in a relieved voice, and looked pointedly at the dresses. 'You'd better put them back, Vicky, and thanks anyway. It was a nice thought on your part,' she tacked on hastily, at the mutinous look in Vicky's eyes.

Vicky walked to the door with Sheena. 'Later,' she said, in a voice that told Sheena that she hadn't given up, and that Sheena might have second thoughts on the matter. Sheena made no attempt to dislodge this forlorn hope. For once she had emerged as the victor, and she was quite content to leave it at that.

As Sheena took a quick shower to freshen herself up before lunch, her thoughts lingered on her earlier conversation with Clay, and again she tried to pinpoint the reason for her uneasy feelings where he was concerned. The trouble was, she conceded silently to herself, she did not know him well enough to be able to gauge his thoughts, and certainly not well enough to know when he was teasing her, or when he meant what he said.

She recalled the amused look in his eyes when he had asked her if she was afraid that he might take advantage of the situation, and what had he said? Her brow wrinkled in thought as she slipped back into her bedroom and searched out a clean blouse, and discarding her jeans, selected a skirt to wear that afternoon. Something about making passionate love to her. Yes, that was it. Her fingers stilled on the zip of the skirt, and she shook her head bewilderedly. What an odd thing for him to have said. He barely knew her, and she him, so what on earth could have prompted him to say something like that?

It was here that she remembered Vicky's comments when they first met, on whether she was Clay's girl-friend, and her brow creased into a deeper frown. At last things were beginning to make sense. Clay Dayman had lots of girl-friends, that much was certain. In fact it was beginning to look as if he was some kind of womaniser!

Her indignation grew as she combed her hair before going down to lunch. Was he afraid that she might join the queue of his admirers? And was that his way of warning her off? She nodded grimly to her reflection in the mirror. So that was what was behind his apparent concern for her welfare. Only it wasn't her welfare he was really worried about, it was his!

No wonder he had brought Doyle into it! Using himself as bait for a possible reconciliation between them. Either way he couldn't lose, she thought scathingly. Her stated intention of broadcasting the news to certain interested parties in the knowledge that Doyle would get to hear about the engagement must have eased his mind considerably, she thought as she left her bedroom and made her way down the stairs and towards the kitchen. It wasn't until she had reached the kitchen door that the thought occurred to her that Clay hadn't appeared particularly pleased at the news—in fact, anything but pleased.

Whether he was pleased or displeased, she couldn't care less, she told herself as she entered the kitchen. She had no intention of contacting anyone at Barter's Ridge, not for that purpose anyway. She would have to let Cookie know that she was all right, and she ought to do that soon, she thought with a pang of conscience for not remembering sooner. It was true that she had only been away for two days, but it felt more like six months! So much had happened.

Vicky was already seated at the table, and helping herself to the salad lunch laid out for them when Sheena joined her, and although she was probably still smarting a little from her defeat over the evening dresses, she gave Sheena a cheerful, 'Hi!' as she sat down.

Clay arrived shortly after Sheena began her lunch, and Vicky gave him a résumé on their exertions on the tennis court and the game of table tennis afterwards, to which he gave a satisfied nod to show that he was pleased that they had been able to amuse themselves.

'We must take Sheena to Coff's Harbour,' he commented to Vicky, who gave a fervent nod at this.

'You'd like that, Sheena,' she said, helping herself to some more salad, prompting the thought from Sheena that whatever else ailed the child, her appetite was a healthy one. 'There's a porpoise pool at Park Beach and they've trained them to do all sorts of things,' she added, and looked at Clay. 'This weekend?' she asked hopefully.

Clay's eyes had been on Sheena, but now he smiled back at Vicky. 'I don't see why not,' he replied airily. 'I'm almost up to date with the office work, and another morning's stint will see the back of it. This weekend it is, then.'

The mention of the weekend brought Vicky's thoughts back to the dinner dance the following evening. 'Sheena hasn't an evening dress to wear for the dinner dance,' she said quickly, darting a look of defiance towards the indignant Sheena. 'So I showed her some of Maria's dresses. They'll fit her, won't they?' she asked Clay.

Sheena's dark look left Vicky and rested on Clay whose thoughtful dark eyes seemed to be measuring her slight figure, and having come to the final measurement, he nodded agreeably. 'There should be no problem there,' he remarked cheerfully.

'As far as size is concerned, no,' replied Sheena, incensed, feeling that she was being ganged up on. 'It's just that——'

Vicky then broke in hastily with, 'She thinks it's a cheek, but I said Maria wouldn't mind, and she won't will she?' she appealed to Clay.

'Considering they were paid for out of my hard-earned cash, I shouldn't think so,' Clay answered, with a twinkle in his dark eyes.

Sheena stared down at her plate. She would be wearing the dress whether she wanted to or not, and she didn't want to wear any of the wretched dresses. It would have been nice, she thought bitterly, to have been able to make a stand somewhere along the line. It wouldn't have occurred to either of these two now watching her closely that she had her pride, and wouldn't feel comfortable in someone else's finery.

'Well?' asked Clay, with a hint of warning in his voice that made her look up quickly at him and take due note of the look in his eyes that plainly said, 'Are you being awkward again?'

Sheena's lips firmed as she met that look with a defiant sparkle in her eyes. 'I'm not sure that any of them will suit me,' she said calmly, although she had wanted to shout it out at him.

'In that case I'll take you into town tomorrow to kit yourself out,' Clay announced firmly.

'I'll come too,' interjected the avidly interested

Vicky, thoroughly enjoying the verbal sparring match between Sheena and Clay, her feminine intuition sensing that there was more behind their too polite responses than met the eye.

Sheena had a horrible suspicion that he had meant what he said, and there was no doubt that Vicky had thought so. 'I don't see why there should be all this fuss over a dress!' she said scathingly. 'I've never dressed up before, and we didn't dress ...' she had been about to say 'at Barter's Ridge', but the look in Clay's eyes stopped her, and she ended lamely with, 'before.'

'At Barter's Ridge, you mean,' replied Clay stiffly, his voice indicating that he was deeply angry. 'Well, you're at Rimini now,' he went on, in a harsh voice that made Vicky open her eyes wide in astonishment and Sheena look away from the fury in his eyes. 'But the situation is somewhat different now, isn't it?' he demanded furiously. 'Here, you are a guest—my guest—and that counts for something around here. You may please yourself, of course, but I would prefer that you dressed in keeping with the rest of my guests for that evening.'

There was an ominous silence after this stern rebuke and Sheena felt as though he had slapped her face. The fact that Vicky looked as shaken as she was did not lessen her fury. Who did he think he was, anyway?

She knew that she was asking for trouble, but she couldn't leave it at that. 'Well, as your guest,' she said, in a too-sugary voice, 'may I request that I be excused from attending?' Her over-bright eyes wavered as they met Clay's.

'Out of the question!' Clay bit back at her savagely. 'You're the reason I'm giving the dinner. Any more objections?' he queried softly, yet warningly.

Sheena swallowed. It was like coming up against a ten-foot wall with spikes! She would go to the dinner, and she would wear an evening dress, and she would enjoy herself! With a distinct feeling that she ought to spring to attention, give a salute, and say, 'No, sir,' she shrugged her slim shoulders in a vain attempt to show that she could not care less either way, and that it was all a fuss over nothing, and replied quietly, 'None,' then reached for the coffee jug, noting with no little surprise how steady her hand was.

Vicky's consoling, 'You'll enjoy it, Sheena, honestly,' did nothing to soothe her inner chagrin at the way Clay had reacted at the mention of Barter's Ridge. She had not meant to make a comparison between Barter's Ridge and Rimini, but he had obviously taken it that way, and had made her feel wretched and ungrateful for all that he had done for her.

That evening she tried on the white dress, accompanied by Vicky and her enthusiastic remarks on how it suited her, she stared at herself in the long mirror. There were no alterations needed, and Sheena had felt a little piqued about this since she was keen to pounce on any excuse as to why she should not wear the dress—or any of the dresses. Not that that would have got her anywhere apart from an embarrassing trip to town as threatened by Clay, to buy clothing.

'It suits you much more that it did Maria,' Vicky commented, as she studied Sheena with her curly head on one side. 'Mum says white doesn't suit every body. I wish she could see you now,' she added, with a suspicion of a break in her voice. She pushed a stray curl back from her forehead as if by that action she could also push back the memories of the past. 'She would suggest that you wear you hair scraped back from the front, with one of those golden bands to keep it back. You know, the Grecian style—and it would suit you. Maria tried it once, but her face was too plump to carry it off properly. Shall I try to find one of those bands for you?' she offered eagerly.

Sheena was too concerned about Vicky's reference to her mother to worry about fashion, and shook her head smilingly. 'I'd never carry it off,' she said simply. 'I feel awkward enough in the dress. I'm not used to dressing up, you know. I shall have enough trouble watching out that I don't trip over the hem.' She glanced down doubtfully at the hem of the full pleated skirt, and took two experimental steps as if dancing.

'There's plenty of leeway,' Vicky remarked, 'even when you're looking down at the hem, and you won't be dancing like that, now will you?' she demanded.

This blunt observation forced a grin from Sheena, who had to concede that she was right.

As she slipped off the dress and changed back into her blouse and skirt, she wondered where Clay was. He had mentioned that he had a lot of phoning around to do that evening in preparation for the impromptu dinner he was giving. She had wanted to phone through to the manager's office at Barter's Ridge and leave a message for Cookie, and she certainly did not want Clay anywhere in earshot, particularly as he seemed to have developed a chip on his shoulder where Barter's Ridge was concerned.

Vicky, it appeared, was also thinking of Clay, though for quite another reason, and she startled Sheena by suddenly asking her, 'You do like Clay, don't you, Sheena? Just a little bit,' she added with a kind of pleading in her eyes.

Sheena's first reaction was to give the blunt reply of, 'No! Not even a little bit!' but the look in Vicky's eyes told her that her answer was important to her. She took a deep breath and rapidly sought for the right words. Words that would not hurt Vicky, yet would help her to understand things from Sheena's point of view.

Seeing her hesitation, Vicky drew her own conclusions. 'Oh, I know he's a bit overbearing at times,' she said, and looked down at her sandalled foot now scuffing the deep pile of the bedroom carpet. 'He's a bit used to having his own way, you see,' she went on carefully. 'But he's not always like that.' She kept her eyes on her swinging foot. 'If I was a little bit older he'd be the kind of man I'd like to marry. He wouldn't ever let you down.'

Sheena looked at her, noticing absently that she wore the same blouse that she had worn the day before, and that it looked in need of a wash. As this thought seeped through to her she felt a spurt of motherly concern for her well-being, and was surprised at her feelings. She had never felt like that over any other child, although she had known many of the station children.

'Only I like you, Sheena,' went on Vicky, unaware of the motherly feelings she had aroused in Sheena. 'And I want things to be right between you and Clay.' She took a quick breath before adding on a cracked note, 'Then I know you'll stay.' She did not say anything else, she did not need to. The next minute she had rushed out of the bedroom, leaving a worried Sheena staring at the closed bedroom door.

If Vicky had repeated her earlier question of did she like Clay, her answer would have been short and very explanatory. Sheena not only disliked him, but at that moment in time, she positively hated him!

Hated him for what he had done to Vicky—making her an accomplice in the bargain. Vicky was in for another cruel disappointment, and she didn't deserve it. Sheena had seen the possibility and the distinct probability of failure, but even she had not contemplated or envisaged the hurt that they would inevitably cause her.

Her hands clenched together tightly. She had hardly known Vicky when the proposal of the mock engagement had first been put forward by Clay, yet she had had her doubts. Clay had known, though, and he must have known full well the risk he was taking in introducing Sheena to the household.

Her nails bit into her palms. Had he hoped to be able to keep her at Rimini? Had that been his plan from the very start? As a companion for Vicky, perhaps? When Sheena thought of the rundown smallholding and the shack she had hoped to make her home, she realised that that must have been when the plan was hatched. He had not thought her capable of running the smallholding, even if she had been able to get it back into shape again. He had also frowned upon the thought of her living alone in what to him must be very primitive conditions.

Her breath expelled slowly. It all added up. She had fallen into his schemes like a ripe plum, and she really hadn't stood a chance. She couldn't walk out on him, she'd nowhere to walk to, but more important than that, she couldn't walk out on Vicky—not now, or at any time that she could envisage in the near future.

Vicky came first, and it was up to Sheena to see that she didn't get hurt. She gave a deep sigh. Soon the time would come when Clay would offer her the post of companion to Vicky, and she would have to accept it. As with all her other dealings with Clay Dayman, she had no choice.

CHAPTER NINE

WHEN Sheena eventually emerged from the bedroom she saw that Vicky's bedroom door was closed, and that meant that she had gone to bed. Her door usually remained open, Sheena had noticed during the day, and she felt a small spurt of relief that she would not have to face her again until breakfast the next morning.

In the hope that Clay had now finished making the round of calls he had said that he would make Sheena slipped down to the lounge, pausing outside Clay's study to ascertain that he was not on the line then hurried through to the lounge to use the extension line.

Although it was out of office hours, she knew that any call would be put through to the manager's flat above the office, as had been done when her father had held the same position.

The call seemed to take a long time to connect through to Barter's Ridge, and as Sheena anxiously held the receiver and waited for the connection, her thoughts inevitably centred on Doyle. The thought that the homestead was only a few yards away from the manager's quarters made her heart thump. What if Doyle just happened to be with the manager? She swallowed. He wouldn't be, she told herself stoutly and if he was, and did answer the call, then she would put the phone down.

She blinked at this thought, slightly surprised at her firm resolve to keep her distance from him. She needed time to think things over. There was no question of her accepting his dubious offer of a flat in Sydney, but the plain fact remained that she was sure that Doyle looked upon her as his property and that, faced with the prospect of losing her for good, would marry her.

No matter how you looked at it, she thought miserably, it all added up to a subtle kind of blackmail, and she wanted no part of it. She could see only too clearly her future as mistress of Barter's Ridge, with Mrs Charter hovering in the background with her too-bright remarks calculated to please Doyle, but her unspoken rebukes and accusing looks would form an unbreakable barrier between them.

Sheena gave a slight shiver. It wasn't a very bright prospect for any of them, and as much as she loved Doyle she couldn't face a future like that.

The connection was then made, and to her vast relief she heard the cheerful voice of Mr Jarvis, the farm manager, answer the call. She gave him her message for Cookie, and said she would be writing to her soon. There was no doubt that the news of her hasty departure had done the rounds of the station and must have caused much speculation, and behind the farm manager's enquiry as to how she liked the North, Sheena could sense his avid curiosity.

She replied that it was early days yet, but she

thought she might well settle there. She wanted to
leave it at that, but Mr Jarvis's, 'Bit sudden, wasn'
it?' comment on her abrupt leaving, gave her no al
ternative but to reply. She stressed the fact that a
Mr Dayman had offered to give her a lift on his way
back up North, she had accepted. There hadn't beer
time, she explained carefully, to do all the rounds o
farewells, particularly as Mr Dayman was anxious t
be off home.

There wasn't much they could make out of that
Sheena told herself as she put the phone down a littl
later. Gossip was rife on the station, just as it was o
any isolated station, and although Cookie woul
keep her counsel on the real reason as to why it had
been necessary for Sheena to leave as abruptly as sh
had, there was nothing to stop others making thei
own deductions, but they would only be guesses, an
none of them would actually know.

The following morning Vicky took Sheena out on
tour of the farm, the nearby dairy premises that was
as the farm ran into several acres of paddocks an
grazing land, too far for a morning trip, even wit
transport.

What had looked like a batch of small white build
ings in the distance turned out to be quite sizeabl
buildings as the girls approached them. Sheena was
little apprehensive as they neared the sectioned-o
dairy sheds. She didn't know the milking times, an
devoutly hoped she wouldn't find herself in th
middle of the herd either coming or leaving the milk
ing sheds.

Vicky laughed as she voiced her fears. 'They won't hurt you,' she said. 'They're just curious, that's all. In any case, milking's over for this morning, they won't be back until this afternoon, and we'll be getting the playroom ready for the dance then, so come on,' she urged Sheena.

When they entered the first shed, Sheena was struck by the almost clinical cleanliness of the large area. Milking machines stood side by side, gleaming like polished silver. The freshly washed floor was immaculately clean and would have done any housewife credit. By the time they had visited the three milking sheds, Sheena realised that this was dairy farming on a very large scale, and was again reminded of Doyle's scathing enquiry to Clay as to whether he ran a smallholding too, and the fact that Clay had held his temper was even more of a marvel to her now.

She had wondered whether they would meet him during their walk about the dairy, but if he was around he did not trouble to show himself, and she had a vague suspicion that he was still displeased with her for attempting to excuse herself from the dinner dance. He had not said a great deal during dinner the previous evening, she recalled, and it would have been an uncomfortable meal had it not been for Vicky's gay chatter that had effectively covered the all-too-frequent bouts of oppressive silences between Sheena and Clay.

Unlike Barter's Ridge, where you were sure to run into several station hands whatever direction you

took on the property, they met very few dairy hands
and those that they did come across were industri
ously engaged in their tasks, and only paused to no(
a welcome to Vicky and her companion, then re
sumed their duties again. It said a lot for the smooth
running of the dairy farm and the use of moder
machinery that so large an industry could be run b
so few hands.

Clay put in a brief appearance for lunch, and be
fore leaving, instructed Vicky not to forget to get th
records out ready for use that evening, and to stay ou
of Pietro's way during the afternoon as he would b
busy preparing the food for the buffet. Would sh
also remember to put some of that chalk stuff on th
playroom floor, ending with, 'Sheena can help you
and that was the only reference to Sheena that h
made; she supposed that she had to be grateful tha
he had remembered her existence!

A highly indignant Vicky had replied that sh
knew what to do, didn't she? and this had brought
slight relaxation of Clay's hard features, and he ha
ruffled her hair in passing her on his way out of th
kitchen.

A slightly mollified Vicky met Sheena's eyes wit
a rueful look in hers. 'He's in a mood,' she said, 'an
he's not usually like that,' she explained to Sheena
'Mum used to say Dad was always having mood
when he was chasing her. I suppose it's something t
do with being in love,' she added half to herself.

Sheena gave a sceptical look at this conversatio
and Vicky correctly interpreted her thoughts. 'The
do too,' she replied assertively, to Sheena's unspoke

rejection of her diagnosis of Clay's unusual manner. 'Didn't your boy-friend have moods?' she demanded of Sheena.

The question threw Sheena, and she blinked. Like her uncle, Vicky had the knack of suddenly discomfiting her when she least expected it. 'No, he did not,' she replied primly, giving Vicky a frown of disapproval at the question.

'Then it wasn't true love,' Vicky replied, with a triumphant note in her voice, totally ignoring the warning signs in Sheena's eyes.

Sheena looked away and stared at the bright blue condiments on the table. 'There are different kinds of love, Vicky,' she said in a low voice, her tone showing her unhappiness at the thoughts the subject had aroused.

'Oh, well,' replied Vicky, now sounding contrite, I suppose so—but it ought to be happy—even if it's moody,' she added obstinately, then abruptly changed the subject. 'Let's offer to do the washing-up for Pietro, that way I'll get in his good books and he'll put me something by later, just in case I miss the pastries.'

After Vicky had ingratiated herself in Pietro's good books, the girls set about getting the playroom ready for the dancing later that evening.

By the time the table tennis board and the various other items of recreation had been stacked away, Sheena saw there was plenty of room for dancing, even with the snooker table still in place at the end of the room.

Seeing her look rest on it, Vicky said, 'Clay covers

that with a special board, just in case someone trie
to use it as a table to rest their drinks on.'

The next task was to search out suitable records fo
dancing, and this Sheena left to Vicky who knev
what would be required, and while Vicky applie
herself to this task, Sheena sprinkled the fine chal
powder over the dancing area.

'I've probably overdone the powder,' she con
mented a little later when all the preparations wer
complete and the girls stood surveying their hand
work. 'Mind you don't slip,' she warned Pietro, as h
walked in carrying the top of a long trestle table tha
would serve as the buffet table, and he altered hi
direction and walked gingerly on the edge of the floo
towards his destination.

All this activity should have taken Sheena's min
off Vicky's disquieting question that had brougl
back memories of her courtship with Doyle, but th
preparations for the coming evening only highlighte
her unhappiness. Doyle had been too sure of her t
indulge in moods, she thought sadly. He was alway
the same, he could be aggressive if opposed, this sh
knew, but then she had never opposed him. He ha
known what he wanted and went straight after it. l
anything it was this quality that she had adored i
him. Uncertain of herself and shy, she had been to
tally overwhelmed by his strength of character.

But there had been one trait of his that she ha
failed to recognise—pride—pride in his name an
standing in the community, and it was this pride tha
had torn them apart.

Her thoughts then centred on Clay Dayman. In a sense they were very alike. Clay Dayman knew what he wanted too, and went after it with the same single-mindedness. He had pride too. Sheena paused on this thought, remembering what he had said about her being his guest, and that counted for something in that locality. Oh, yes, she thought bitterly. He had just as much pride as Doyle, and yet he had con-demned Doyle for the way he had treated her after her father had absconded with the station payroll.

How would he have acted in a similar situation? she wondered ironically. It was all very well to judge others, but it hadn't happened to him, and he had no right at all to condemn Doyle. She totally ignored the small voice deep within her that insisted that a man like Clay Dayman would not have acted as Doyle had. If he had loved the woman involved, then no amount of skulduggery would have swerved him from his course. That small voice was just acting in a spirit of fair play, and needn't necessarily be right, and Sheena did not want to think of Clay as being a better person than Doyle. For one thing, he was older than Doyle, of that she was certain, and age always, or should always, give a person that much more wis-dom. The three or four years that she suspected that Clay could give Doyle would have made all the dif-ference, and would have undoubtedly made him see things from Sheena's point of view rather than follow-ing the dictates of his fierce pride.

Having reached this conclusion, Sheena should have felt better about things, yet she didn't, for that

small voice that kept interrupting her trend of
thought told her that she was a fool if she believed
that things could have been different. If that was so
what was she doing at Rimini, a dairy farm miles
away from Barter's Ridge, and miles away from the
folk she had grown up with? There was such a thing
as fate, that small voice persisted. She was meant to
be here, so she might just as well accept it and not
keep harping back to the past.

Vicky helped her dress for the dinner dance that
evening, and although Sheena would have preferred
to be on her own, she hadn't the heart to refuse her
help. She so obviously missed feminine company.
With her mother and grandmother, plus two aunts, it
must have been a female-dominated household once
upon a time, and there would have been plenty of
gaiety and bustle about the old homestead in those
days. It was perhaps this atmosphere that Sheena had
caught when she had first arrived at Rimini, as if the
old place was now hushed and expectant, ready to
expand once again with the noise and laughter of
children.

Sheena had just successfully fended off Vicky's
offer to 'make her up', smilingly refusing the use of a
well stocked make-up case, that she suspected had
belonged to her mother, when the first guests arrived
and Vicky rushed out to the landing to get a bird's
eye view of the first arrivals.

'It's Cynthia,' she said flatly, as she returned to join
Sheena. 'Might have known she'd be the first. Hopes
to get Clay on his own, I bet,' she added sagely, and

then rushed away again as another car could be heard drawing up outside the homestead.

'That was Mr and Mrs Dawson,' she reported, a few moments later. 'They've got the nearest farm along the valley, and Daphne and Jeannie are dressed up to kill,' she giggled at her own wit. 'Cynthia will be furious,' she added in a pleased voice. 'Daphne's wearing deep red too, only a shade lighter, and the shades will clash. She'll spend the evening avoiding standing next to her.'

There was another crunch of wheels on the drive, and Vicky was off again. This time she returned with wide eyes. 'You've got some competition tonight, Sheena,' she announced breathlessly. 'There's three of Clay's exes in that lot. Oh, I do wish I could be a fly on the wall! Mandy Johnson and Cynthia loathe the sight of one another, mainly because of Clay, of course. He used to date them alternately, just to show that there were no hard feelings, but there were, of course—between them, that was, they each thought they'd hooked him.'

Sheena stared at her. She couldn't be serious, surely? 'What exactly do you mean by Clay's exes?' she asked, her voice petering out faintly as she envisaged the evening ahead of her.

'I told you,' replied Vicky impatiently, as she smoothed a pleat of the white dress back into place as if Sheena was about to model the gown. 'Also-rans,' she supplied irreverently, 'and I'll bet that's why Clay's asked them. As soon as the party season starts, he's pestered with invitations from hopeful parents with good-looking daughters.'

'Vicky!' exclaimed Sheena, shocked at her bald observations. 'You're making your uncle sound like a heartless man. If I believed you, I'd feel very sorry for the poor girls he's apparently led up the garden path.'

'They practically dragged him up it,' replied the unrepentant Vicky, with a wide grin.

'There's nothing like that kind of treatment to give a man a swollen head,' answered Sheena sourly. 'No wonder he's used to having his own way!'

'Clay hasn't got a swollen head!' Vicky retorted smartly. 'It's not his fault if they throw themselves at him. Besides, he's rich, isn't he?' she added with honest simplicity.

'Then he shouldn't encourage them,' Sheena snapped back, feeling outraged.

'Why shouldn't he?' challenged Vicky. 'They deserve all they get, they're only after his money.'

'Not all of them, surely?' Sheena said faintly, feeling out of her depth.

'Well, most of them,' conceded Vicky. 'There's Daphne and Jeannie for a start. Their father's farm needs a lot of money poured into it to keep it going. You know about Cynthia, she's coming to the end of her modelling days. There's Mandy Johnson, whose mother's a widow with expensive tastes and hasn't any...'

Sheena did not wait to hear any more, but made her way to the door, pausing only long enough to snatch a handkerchief out of the dressing table drawer, then with a firm but resolute, 'Goodnight, Vicky!' she went to join the gathering below stairs.

Her heart was hammering against her ribs as she entered the lounge where the guests were assembled, and where Pietro was handing out glasses of sherry before dinner was announced.

She felt rather than saw the curious looks directed her way at her entry, but she looked directly at Clay, who seemed to be taking his time in his approval at her appearance and her apparel. She saw him give a small smile, and then walk towards her. 'Meet Sheena, everybody,' he announced, with an inflection in his voice that spoke of ownership, and that made her give him a wary look.

Vicky had not been all that far out in her surmising of the number of guests invited. There were in fact nine. To Sheena, as she was introduced to them one by one, it seemed a much larger gathering, and she was relieved when that part of the evening was over and she could relax.

Mr and Mrs Dawson were a pleasant, if slightly garrulous, couple, but there were undertones of anxiety in their too-bright welcome to Sheena. There was no sign of restriction, moneywise, where the female contingency's dresses were concerned, Sheena noticed, for although she did not know much about fashion, she did know an expensive dress when she saw one, and it did occur to her that perhaps Mr Dawson might not have had quite such a hard time of it if he had been able to curtail his family's dress allowances.

As these thoughts went through Sheena's mind, she rebuked herself sternly. It was all Vicky's fault. She ought not to have taken any notice of what she had said, but like her uncle, she had an uncomfortable way of getting right to the heart of the matter and presenting the bare facts without frills.

Jeannie and Daphne Dawson had also given her an effusive welcome, but their smiles did not reach their eyes, and Sheena had an astute feeling that should she find herself alone in their company, the welcome would not have been quite so evident. This was not so surprising, considering that they looked upon her as an encroachment in their bid to reimburse the family fortune.

When she was introduced to Mrs Johnson and her daughter Mandy, Sheena again wished that Vicky had not been so forthcoming in her bald summing-up. Mrs Johnson's grip had been noticeably slack when she had taken Sheena's hand, and her inquisitive eyes had seemed to bore right into her. Mandy Johnson, a very pretty redhead with blue eyes, bore no resemblance to her mother, and must, Sheena presumed, have taken after her father in looks. She appeared shy and diffident, but as Vicky had intimated, there was nothing shy or diffident in the look that Sheena caught her directing at Cynthia, when Cynthia stationed herself beside Clay as dinner was announced.

It could have been embarrassing as Cynthia showed no intention of standing aside and letting Clay lead Sheena into the dining room, but Clay forestalled what could have been a nasty moment by standing by the dining room door and politely ushering his guests in.

Sheena found herself seated on Clay's right hand, with Mr Dawson opposite. Cynthia sat next to Sheena, and next to her sat Daphne, her bright red dress in direct contrast to Cynthia's crimson one. Vicky had been right when she had said that the two shades would clash, and they did, Sheena thought absently as they settled at the table.

Mandy sat next to Mr Dawson, and directly opposite Cynthia, and Sheena foresaw a very jolly gathering in which the normal fare might very well be replaced by saucers of cream for the antagonists in the coming battle of the sexes.

With Cynthia intent on re-establishing herself in Clay's affections, and adopting the role of a frequent visitor's right to put the other guests at their ease, she rather overdid her attention to Sheena, who was made to feel like the last-minute entry in the field of runners, and had to be shown the finishing line!

It wasn't long before the talk centred on Vicky, with Mrs Dawson solicitously enquiring if she had come to terms with her loss yet, and Clay's guarded reply that he had hopes in that direction, his dark eyes resting on Sheena as he said this, making Sheena apply herself hastily to her food.

'The child needs a mother,' said Mrs Johnson, her eyes resting fondly on her daughter as she voiced the subtle suggestion.

Cynthia's eyes narrowed at this. 'Oh, she's already chosen one, hasn't she, Clay?' she said sweetly, giving

Mandy a look of loathing. 'But as we all know Vicky's state of mind at the present time, she's quite liable to form sudden attachments,' she added, this time favouring Sheena with a challenging look.

Clay's cold eyes rested briefly on Cynthia. 'Vicky's as sane as you and I,' he said coldly. 'The fact that she is unable to admit her loss doesn't make her an idiot.'

Cynthia's hurried, 'I didn't mean to make it sound like that, Clay. You must know that,' she pleaded.

'She just needs understanding, that's all,' inserted Mandy, giving Clay a sympathetic smile to show that she realised how hard it must be for him to cope alone with such a problem.

'Well, whatever it is,' snapped Cynthia, making a swift recovery from her melting act, 'Sheena appears to have the right touch, don't you, Sheena?' she asked her spitefully.

Sheena looked up to find all eyes upon her, and her wide eyes appealed for help from Clay.

He did not let her down, and gave her a slow heart-stopping smile. 'And that only goes to prove that there's nothing wrong with Vicky's mental calculations,' he said softly, making Sheena's cheeks turn a rosy hue. 'I happen to feel the same way myself,' he added quietly.

During the slight hush that followed Clay's endorsement of Sheena's virtues, Sheena was certain that everyone must hear her thumping heart, and her indignant eyes clashed with Clay's dark ones. It was as if he had made a public declaration of love, he thought distractedly, and wondered how she was xpected to get through the rest of the evening as she ensed the gathering of hostile forces around her. She wallowed. That was something else she had learned bout Clay Dayman: he didn't bother to do things by alves!

'So it's off with the old and on with the new, is it?' Cynthia asked Sheena, with narrowed eyes.

Sheena stared back at her, not understanding the question, but Clay did. 'I'm afraid the station boss is till ahead on points,' he replied softly, his eyes on he now furious Sheena, who glared back at him. How dared he bring Doyle into this! She was only thankful that she was miles away from Barter's Ridge, and that only she and Clay knew who he was eferring to.

Cynthia's eyes remained fixed on Sheena, and ook due note of her flushed cheeks and accusing yes as she looked back at Clay. 'So he's a station oss, is he? You do fly high, don't you? I must study our technique,' she added meaningly.

'It isn't anything to do with technique,' Clay growled ominously, with a warning note to Cynthia o watch her step. 'It's what you are that counts, not vhat you try to make yourself into. This is real life, ot the modelling world.' He glanced around the able, instantly dismissing Cynthia from his mind. 'If everyone's finished, I suggest we move into the games oom and let Pietro get on with the clearing up,' he aid abruptly.

Sheena found herself unable to look at Cynthia as

the company left the dining table and moved toward
the games room. She had not enjoyed the dinner an
had little hope of enjoying the rest of the evening
entertainment.

Seven women and two men—it was ridiculous! sh
thought, as she tried to envisage the portly Mr Daw
son attempting to keep pace with the demands tha
would be made upon him when the dancing startec
It also occurred to her that there must be a shortag
of male escorts in that area. She glanced towards th
end of the games room at Clay, now busy puttin
some records on, his lean dark features emphasisin
his Italian heredity. She drew a deep breath. He wa
as dark as Doyle was fair, but both men knew how t
enslave hearts, she thought bitterly, and reversed he
earlier thoughts. There were probably plenty c
escorts, but few eligible bachelors—eligible, that wa;
from the material point of view.

At this point two young men strolled in to join th
company, and at Clay's dry, 'I thought you weren'
going to make it,' gave profuse apologies for thei
late arrival.

'It was Bob's fault,' said the taller of the two, wit'
a wide grin. 'Our team won, and he got dragged int
the celebrations.'

'Only the drinking,' replied his companion, an
stared hopefully towards the side of the room wher
the trestle table had been put ready to hold the col
buffet later. 'I'm starving,' he announced gloomily.

'Then you'll have to snatch a sandwich on you
way round the floor,' replied Clay unsympatheticall

out he had a twinkle in his eye. 'Pietro should be filling that space up any time now.' He then looked directly at Sheena. 'Meet Bob Tester and Jack Milton, Sheena, our local rugger heroes. I ought to have known better than to invite them to dinner when Newcastle was visiting Bellingen,' he added with a grin.

The addition of two nice-looking, healthy males made the party a much more bearable proposition from Sheena's point of view, since she had had visions of being swept on to the dance floor by Clay, followed by envious looks from the rest of the females left to tap their heels to the rhythm of the music.

During the course of the evening, she learned that Bob was a distant cousin of Mandy's, and judging by the wistful looks he sent Mandy's way, Sheena was sure that he was in love with her, and not too sure that his feelings weren't reciprocated by Mandy, although she might have been putting on an act to impress upon Clay the fact that she had other admirers. Sheena hoped not, as she liked the look of Bob.

If Bob had an interest in Mandy, his friend Jack certainly had an eye on Cynthia. That they had met at many parties was evident by Cynthia's casual acceptance of his company, and her, 'Don't you dare try and dance with me with that wedge in your hand,' referring to a thick sandwich that he held and that he had evidently got round Pietro to supply him with as Pietro had only just begun to fill up the buffet table.

Now that the numbers were more even, the danc ing got under way, and the men took turns in part nering each of the girls in turn so that no one felt lef out.

The general atmosphere too had lightened, and even Cynthia seemed to be enjoying herself in spite of Clay's crushing comment at dinner. That she had forgiven him was obvious by the way she clung to him when they danced together.

As Sheena happened to be sitting that dance out she could not help but notice this, and she almos blushed at Cynthia's shameless approach to the man who only a day ago had bluntly told her he had los interest in her.

That was love, she thought bitterly; there was a different set of values where love was concerned, and she wondered how she would react if Doyle were to suddenly walk into the room and hold out his arms to her, as he had done before. Would she calmly walk out on the dance floor with him? Or would she fling herself into his arms, and cling to him as Cyn thia was attempting to do in Clay's arms?

If Doyle had acted as Clay was now doing, deter minedly extracting himself from the clinging Cyn thia at every opportunity offered, Sheena would die of shame. She would be heartbroken, but she would have enough pride left to salvage her dignity.

When Clay claimed the next dance with her Sheena's spirits were low. She ought not to have thought of Doyle, but the soft popular dance music of the day had inevitably awakened memories she badly needed to forget.

'Thinking of your beloved?' queried Clay, as he swung her into the tempo of the dance.

Sheena could have hit him. He had an instinctive sense for the truth where she was concerned, and as usual he was right. She gulped, and looked away from his searching eyes, attempting to concentrate on her steps and keeping in pace with her partner.

'So you were!' he commented conversationally. 'Did he hold you like this?' he asked roughly, as he pulled her closer to him, so close that she could feel his breath fanning her forehead.

Sheena made an attempt to pull herself away from him, although she knew that several pairs of eyes were on them, but she was past caring. If he wanted her co-operation he had better stop baiting her.

'Backing out again?' he asked, in a savage whisper against her hair, as his arm around her back became a steel rod that held her closer to him.

Sheena's lovely eyes echoed her feelings as she met Clay's hard ones. 'Leave Doyle out of this, if you please!' she answered in a low vibrant whisper.

'That's not so easy, is it?' he replied softly. 'Not while you have that look in your eyes.'

Sheena decided to forget that remark. She had done her best to join in the gaiety of the evening and had, she thought, succeeded, until now. 'I'm having a lovely time,' she said through clenched teeth, trying to dispel the panic she was beginning to feel at his closeness. 'Why must you spoil things?' she asked crossly, taking refuge in fury because she could not understand what was happening to her, she felt weak and suddenly helpless against this strong, vibrant man.

'Because you're not trying hard enough,' he replied harshly, his mouth close to her ear so that no one else could hear. 'Forget yourself, and think of Vicky sitting up there on the stairs watching us. If this tune brings back memories to you, so it does to her—it was her parents' favourite.'

Her wide lovely eyes now held contrition in them as they met Clay's grim ones. 'I'm sorry,' she said in a low voice. 'That was selfish of me. But please don't make any more references to the past, it isn't very helpful,' she added pleadingly.

Clay's hard look softened as his eyes searched hers, noting the way her wide eyes appeared as pools of blue sparkling water, and suddenly he bent and kissed her hard, but said nothing.

The rest of the dance passed by in a semi-haze for Sheena, who could still feel the touch of his lips on hers, and something else that she could not define and was afraid to even try.

CHAPTER TEN

THE rest of that week passed by with Sheena in a bewildered haze at the rapidity of events following the night of the dance.

She knew that her engagement to Clay would come as no surprise to the neighbouring homesteads. Clay had seen to that by kissing her on the dance floor, deliberately choosing the time and the place to create just such an illusion.

Cynthia, Sheena remembered, had left shortly afterwards, and Mr and Mrs Dawson had become even more chatty during the rest of the evening. After what Mrs Johnson considered a decent interval after Cynthia's departure, she and Mandy also left, with Mrs Johnson firmly refusing Bob's offer of escort. Jack's attempt to leave with Cynthia had also received short shrift by a barely polite Cynthia.

All this Sheena had noticed in an abstracted haze as if she were in a play, and the other actors were acting out their roles and that part of the play had nothing to do with her.

Now that the audience had left, Sheena had hoped that things would return to some level of normality, but she was dismayed to find that Clay had suddenly adopted a very possessive attitude towards her, much to Vicky's delight and Sheena's discomfort.

She had to keep reminding herself that he had warned her of the line that he was going to take, and that she ought not to worry over a certain look in his eyes when they rested on her—or the way he had casually taken her arm the day he showed her over the rest of the property.

It was all for Vicky's benefit, she told herself sternly when her knees started to turn to jelly at his slightest touch. After that brief but devastating kiss on the dance floor, he had abided by his promise not to force his attentions on her, but there was a look in his eyes at times that had reached out to her and was stronger than any physical action, and bewildered her by its intensity.

A few days before the proposed outing to Coff's Harbour, Clay received a letter from a friend of his telling him of the death of a colleague of theirs in Newcastle. The fact that the funeral was taking place that weekend meant that the outing would have to be postponed until the following weekend.

Vicky had taken the news without any show of disappointment, stating that she and Sheena could find plenty to do while Clay was away for the weekend.

For Sheena it meant a welcome break from Clay's dominant presence that was threatening to completely engulf her existence. Her thoughts no longer centred on Doyle, she was too enmeshed in the present to have any time for the past.

As for Vicky's troubles, the ploy of distracting her from her makebelieve world had been totally successful, for not one reference to her parents had been made since the night of the dance, makebelieve or otherwise.

On the odd occasion when Sheena's thoughts had gone back to Barter's Ridge, she felt that she had been living in a dream world and that Doyle had been the fairy prince on whom she had built her hopes and dreams, but now she was back to reality with real-life people with real-life problems. On this thought she recalled what Clay had said to Cynthia, and how right he had been. She sighed deeply. She was back to Clay again!

Just as Sheena had convinced herself that all was well with Vicky, Vicky had a relapse. It happened that weekend when Clay was away in Newcastle, brought on by a visit of Cynthia's, ostensibly to collect some records she had lent Clay some time ago. Sheena had suspected that there was another purpose behind the visit, made at a time when Clay would normally be home and free from any duty he usually carried out in his working week. Since Vicky had come to live with him, he had made a point of leaving his weekends free, and this fact was well known around the neighbourhood.

When Cynthia found that Clay was away and only the girls were there, she took her frustration out on them, verbally attacking first Sheena and then Vicky, as she flew to Sheena's defence when she accused Sheena of playing with Clay's affections and making him look a fool, and why didn't she go back south again where she belonged, and marry that other man she was supposed to be in love with?'

Sheena was still working out her reply to this to tally unfair accusation when Vicky flung herself into the fray with, 'It's none of your business, Cynthia Layton. And Clay's not a fool!' she added vehemently. 'He would have been if he'd married you!' she tacked on furiously.

Sheena gave a gasp at this bald comment. 'Vicky!' she exclaimed in a horrified voice. 'That was most uncalled-for!' she admonished her.

'Well, she shouldn't have started it,' replied the unrepentant Vicky. 'She's making out that Clay would have married her if you hadn't come along and it's not true. Just because he had a few dates with her, it doesn't mean anything, only she's trying to make out it did.'

'How do you know?' snapped Cynthia, now beyond all reasoning. 'What do you know about it? You're just a spoilt brat that took a dislike to me sight, and what's happened is all your fault.' She glared at Sheena. 'You can count yourself lucky that she took to you—if she hadn't, you'd have been thrown on to the scrap heap as well. He's got some crazy idea that she comes first. He feels sorry for her because she's lost her parents, and she plays on it making out that they're still alive. That way she gets more notice taken of her——'

At this point Vicky flung herself at Cynthia with flailing fists and murderous intentions.

Only Sheena's swift intervention prevented an all-out fight, and holding Vicky back from Cynthia she asked her to leave, her cold voice conveyed that she wouldn't be responsible for her safety if she stayed.

For a split second it looked as if Cynthia would stand her ground, but she evidently decided that discretion was better than valour and turning on her spiked heels she walked slowly to the door and out of the homestead.

Sheena gave Vicky a swift hug before she released her, and attempting to bring a light note into the affair said, 'She forgot her records.'

When Vicky turned to face her, Sheena was shocked by the look of dumb misery in her eyes as she said dully, 'Yes.' That was all she said, and started to make a dash for the door.

'Vicky!' called the worried Sheena. 'Don't take any notice of her. She didn't really mean what she said. She thinks she's in love with Clay, and she's very unhappy, can't you see that?'

Vicky did not reply but continued in her headlong rush to the door, leaving Sheena staring at the patterned carpet at her feet and wishing with all her heart that Clay was there. Instinctively she knew that she must leave Vicky alone, because nothing she could say would help her at that time. She had to get over it in her own way, but this thought did not stop Sheena from feeling utterly helpless and totally useless.

One other fact stood out in stark reality. Clay's engagement ploy would no longer work. Vicky was too astute not to see through it now. Cynthia had very effectively opened her eyes to this possibility, and it

would not take her very long to work out the facts
for herself.

Sheena gave a deep sigh. Where would that leave
her? In all probability, hating her and Clay for their
part in the plot.

Her hands clenched by her side. It was all so un
fair, as if Vicky hadn't enough to contend with with
out having to watch while another part of her world
collapsed around her, which it would when Sheena
left Rimini.

At this thought she shook her head, as if to throw
off this unwelcome conclusion. She didn't want to
leave Rimini, and she couldn't understand why. No
so very long ago, she had wished that she could just
walk out and leave the Daymans to their own machi
nations, since it appeared that they were quite
capable of managing their own affairs without her
help.

It was not as if anything had changed, she told
herself firmly, although she had to concede that
Vicky's behaviour had definitely improved during
the last week, and there had been no tantrums, no
since the first day of her arrival.

It was Sheena's company, of course, that had made
such a difference to Vicky's environment, and Clay
had gambled on the possibility that Vicky would take
to Sheena. Sheena's lips twisted at this thought, re
calling Cynthia's bald comment of her being thrown
out on to the scrap heap if the gamble had not come
off.

As much as this thought hurt, she had to admit the

truth of it. If Vicky had spurned her company, that shack would have been built in record time and Sheena hustled out of Rimini at the earliest possible opportunity.

It was here that a thought hit her that made her open her eyes wide in consternation. If Cynthia had opened Vicky's eyes to the truth, so she had opened Sheena's to the distinct and frightening possibility that she was not going to be allowed to leave Rimini!

Her knees were weak as she walked to the nearest chair and sat down on it. She had underestimated Clay all along the line! He had presented the engagement as a ploy to keep her at Rimini. She swallowed hard. It wouldn't have looked very good if he had offered her the post of companion to Vicky when she had first arrived, although clearly that had been what he had in mind—not after her firm assertion that she wanted a home of her own. She nodded her head slowly in confirmation. That was when the false engagement idea had been born. Her lovely eyes misted over. Somewhere along the line his thinking had changed, and she knew without a doubt that he meant to go through with the whole thing!

Quite suddenly everything became clear to her. The way he had deliberately set out to capture her heart. Her breath caught on a raw sob. He knew only too well how to go about that. She was not a vain girl, but she was not blind either. She knew that she had the looks to attract men—look what had happened with Doyle, she told herself bitterly.

Clay must have been attracted too, but it didn't go

any further than that, and she would be a fool if she thought otherwise. Vicky needed feminine companionship, someone old enough to watch over her, and Sheena Greig of no fixed address fitted the bill admirably! That Vicky had immediately taken to her must have been an added bonus for Clay, and from that moment on she hadn't stood a chance!

She wondered how long he intended to give her before she was dragged up the aisle. As clearly as she had suddenly perceived the truth behind his recent attentiveness, she saw just as clearly the future he had lined up for her. Love had no place in his reasoning, she thought wildly, as she envisaged the misery such a marriage would bring her. When she remembered his casual comments at the dinner table that night when he had said that the station boss was still ahead on points, her blood ran cold. That was precisely the way he had looked upon her attachment to Doyle, and an attachment that had to be severed before his plans reached a successful conclusion.

She gulped. No wonder he had been upset at her mention of Barter's Ridge, almost to the point of turning positively savage when he thought that she was making comparisons between the two properties.

What if she let Doyle have her address, and he came to collect her? she wondered. What could Clay Dayman do about that? Precisely nothing! she thought stoutly. A slight frown appeared on her smooth forehead, as she remembered something else. Hadn't Clay suggested that she do just that? Holding the possibility of a reunion between them as a carrot to gain her co-operation.

The frown disappeared as she reminded herself that that was before he had had a change of mind and had rearranged his plans for her future. She also distinctly remembered the answer she had given him when the subtle suggestion had first been mooted. She had said that she had no intention of contacting Doyle, and she had meant it.

She shook her head sadly. She still meant it. There was no future for her at Barter's Ridge. That part of her life was over and done with.

She got up shakily from the chair and walked slowly towards the lounge and out into the garden. She knew what she must do, and she must do it that evening when Clay returned from Newcastle.

Just for once, she told herself miserably, she had to stand her ground and make him see how impossible the whole charade had become. She would not let him know that she was now fully aware of his plans for her future, she couldn't have borne him to know that, for if he tried to persuade her to his way of thinking he would soon find out something that she was desperate to keep from him. So she was a fool, and had once again fallen in love with the wrong man. Doyle had been wrong for her. She knew that now, just as she knew that she had never really been in love with him. She had fallen for his looks and his autocratic outlook, but that was all.

She had been able to forget Doyle, but she would never forget Clay. It would have been so easy, she thought miserably, to have allowed herself to be carried away on the tide of his will, to know that she would be near him for the rest of time, but now she was able to understand a little more about pride. She had pride, and it was this pride that would save her from giving way to her foolish heart.

One day Clay would meet the woman destined to steal his heart, and Sheena would have to stand on the sidelines and helplessly watch his inward turmoil, tied to a woman he did not love and having to turn away from the one he did love. That he would stand by his word Sheena had no doubts whatsoever, and because he was that kind of man she had to prevent him from ruining both their lives.

It would not be easy for her during the next few months, but if she could persuade Clay to her way of thinking, and he agreed to her leaving, but still keeping in close contact with Vicky, then it could all work out in time, and she wouldn't feel that she had let either of them down.

She ate a solitary meal that evening. Pietro had taken Vicky up a tray of food that she had scarcely touched, Sheena noticed, when he brought it back later.

There was no point in Sheena attempting to see Vicky, or to try and talk her out of her misery. She knew where she could find Sheena, and it was best left at that.

While Sheena waited for Clay's return that evening, she had to force herself to sit quietly in the lounge and not keep rushing to the windows each time she thought she heard the car engine. She had to stay calm, she told herself. It wasn't going to be easy putting her views across as it was, and would be far more difficult if she rushed her fences.

It was just after eight when she heard the sound she had been waiting to hear for what had seemed like hours, then she heard the deep voice of Clay as he spoke to Pietro in the kitchen.

Somehow she made herself stay where she was, and quickly picked up a magazine to give the impression that she had been reading when he arrived. The nasty thought that he might decide to go straight to his study, a normal habit of his, to check up on the farm news during his absence, then occurred to her, and she was on the point of heading him off when he met her at the door of the lounge.

'All quiet on the western front?' he queried, with a lift of those expressive brows of his, and making her heart contract.

'I'm afraid not,' she managed to say calmly, although her **heart was** thumping as his dark eyes bored into hers.

'Vicky?' he said quietly. 'What happened? I thought we were winning on that front,' he commented thoughtfully.

Sheena took a deep breath. It was now or never! 'Something happened today,' she said slowly, making herself look away from Clay's searching eyes. 'Something that proved that our little distraction isn't going to work,' she went on steadily, still refusing to meet his eyes. She swallowed. 'And it proved to me that we'd be doing more harm than good, although,' she amended quickly, 'I think the harm's already been done.'

She stole a quick glance at Clay who was now watching her with narrowed eyes and a firmness about his mouth that made her quail inside. The entrance of Pietro with a tray of coffee and sandwiches for Clay, prevented any more conversation until his departure, then Clay said abruptly, 'Well?' impatiently waiting for Sheena to go on.

Sheena swallowed again. Then she launched into Cynthia's visit. She didn't like telling tales, but there was no other way to make him understand how it was, ending with, 'She as good as told Vicky that we were putting on a show for her benefit—oh, not in so many words,' she amended slowly, 'but Vicky's astute enough to understand what she was getting at.' She hesitated. 'She went straight to her room, and I haven't seen her since,' she said steadily. 'Under the circumstances, I think it would be better if we dropped the whole idea,' she added firmly, then looked up at him. 'I've been thinking of another way in which we might help her—in fact, the only way in which I can help,' she tacked on determinedly, and went on to outline her plan.

'I don't know how soon you can get the shack rebuilt,' she commented persistently, in spite of the warning lights in Clay's eyes that had been there since she had told him that she intended to carry out her original plan of making a go of working up her father's smallholding into a viable business again. 'Vicky can help,' she told him. 'It will be the very thing to take her mind off her troubles,' she said, trying to inject a note of enthusiasm into her voice, for the thought had just struck her that she might need the same remedy.

Clay, it appeared, was not thinking of Vicky, but Sheena. 'And what do you intend to do with yourself in the evenings?' he queried harshly. 'Sit and mope and think of what might have been if your father hadn't let you down? You wouldn't have the sense to see that someone else might want to make you happy, you're too tied up with the past to see that, aren't you?' he demanded savagely.

Sheena felt as if he had slapped her hard. She was trying to give him a way out, and he didn't want one. He was not used to having his well-laid plans upset. He was probably, she conceded miserably, thinking of the gossip her leaving Rimini would cause, particularly after that little demonstration he had given on the dance floor. She lifted her chin. But then he had covered himself there, hadn't he, by bringing in Doyle as a contender?

If he wanted to think that she was still in love with Doyle, then let him think so. It would be easier in the long run, she told herself wearily. He could hardly go ahead with his plans if she was in love with someone else. She stood up abruptly. 'It's been a long day,' she said, her weariness plainly showing in her voice.

'Running away again?' Clay said harshly. 'Well, perhaps it's just as well. Right now I'd like to shake some sense into you, but I doubt if it would make any difference. I guess I expected too much of you, too soon.' This was said on a tired-sounding note, and made her glance back at him quickly.

Her eyes met his as she hesitated. She wanted to tell him that she was not ungrateful for all that he had done for her, but he had a certain look in his eyes that told her that he would not appreciate such a sentiment at that time. 'Just because you've got a chip on your shoulder about your father, you don' have to take it out on the rest of us,' he added grimly

Sheena swallowed hard. 'I have not got a chip on my shoulder,' she replied stiffly, blinking back the tears that were threatening to spill over. 'Not about my father, or anyone. I was just trying to help the only w-way I can——' She could not say more, for the tears were now cascading down her cheeks, and she made a dash for the door and the safety of her bedroom.

CHAPTER ELEVEN

SHEENA had only just entered her bedroom when Vicky joined her, and stood looking at her as if uncertain what to say to her.

Her eyes were swollen with crying over a long period, and her off-white blouse was now definitely grubby. Sheena, who had been about to indulge in her own bout of tears, forgot her troubles as she gazed at Vicky.

'Did you hate your father?' Vicky asked, a slight hiccup intervening between the words.

Sheena's eyebrows went up as she considered this extraordinary question, and wondered what had prompted Vicky to ask it. Vicky's next words, however, enlightened her.

'I heard what Clay said to you,' she said, fixing her red-rimmed eyes on the floor. 'I didn't mean to listen, but I couldn't help it,' she explained carefully. Then her voice was caught in a low sob as she rushed on, 'I hated my father and my mother for leaving me alone. For not coming back for me—and they're not coming back, Sheena,' she added on an almost hysterical note. 'They're never coming back. I didn't want to believe it, but it's true. Clay said it was, but I wouldn't believe him.' Her small frame racked with another rasping sob.

Sheena held out her arms to her. 'Don't torture yourself, Vicky,' she said gently. 'I know it's not easy, but at least you've been brave enough to face up to it now.'

Vicky gave a loud sniff and threw herself into Sheena's arms. ' I couldn't tell anyone else,' she got out as a fresh bout of weeping broke out, and she buried her curly head in Sheena's shoulder. 'I didn't cry before,' she said in between gasping sobs, 'but now I can't stop.'

'You go ahead and have your cry,' Sheena told her soothingly, 'it sometimes helps to ease the pain. It's a remedy I've often tried and can recommend.'

A short while later Clay, who had obviously been searching for Vicky, looked in on Sheena and found Vicky fast asleep on Sheena's bed, with Sheena sitting beside the bed still holding the sleeping girl's hand.

The question was in his eyes as they met hers, and she nodded. 'She's all right now,' she said in a low voice. 'She'll be a bit weepy for a day or so, but at least she's got it out of her system.'

Clay nodded abruptly, then lifted the sleeping Vicky gently off Sheena's bed and carried her back to her own room.

With Vicky's recovery, a truce seemed to have been made between Clay and Sheena. It was as if by mutual consent they had abandoned their differences caused by Sheena's decision to leave Rimini.

The days slipped by with Vicky making great strides towards a total recovery. There would still be imes when she had a suspicion of a tear in her black yes, but Sheena and Clay, being on the lookout for uch occasions, soon jolted her out of her depression.

The proposed trip to Coff's Harbour took place the ollowing weekend, and Sheena enjoyed listening to Vicky's exuberant exclamations at the antics of the orpoises at Park Beach. 'Did you see that!' she vould call out to Sheena time and time again.

Sheena would have enjoyed it all a lot better if she iad not been constantly aware of Clay's eyes upon ier, and feeling once again the mesmeric hold of hose dark enigmatic eyes of his. Just what did he vant of her? she would wonder silently. Vicky was iow completely back to normal, and there was now io real reason why she should continue to stay on at Rimini.

She knew that she was a coward, for she had re-rained from bringing up the subject of her moving out to her father's smallholding. She felt that the next nove was up to Clay. He knew her sentiments in this, and as each week slipped by she found herself waiting to hear that the shack had been rebuilt and was ready for her occupation.

By the time a month had gone by, with no such communication from Clay, she finally got the mess-ige that nothing was being done about the shack, and that Clay had no intention of letting her carry out her wish for total independence.

Sheena could no longer allow herself to hope for release from the bitter-sweet trap she had so inno-cently walked into. Each day brought her into close

contact with Clay, even closer contact than she had
had with Doyle, for at Barter's Ridge it was Sheena
who would surreptitiously watch Doyle, longing for
a sign that he still cared for her—a sign that he had
been very careful not to provide.

At Rimini, it was Clay who would watch Sheena
and it was Sheena who would raise the barrier between them. It was a complete reverse from the past
but for very different reasons.

By now Clay had given her her father's savings
and the amount was certainly enough to keep her going until she had decided what she was going to do.
Without Clay's help she knew she would stand no
chance of making the smallholding a success. It
would have helped if she had had some idea of how
to proceed, but she had none, and there was no one
else that she could turn to for advice.

Her disappointment over his refusal to co-operate
in this was soon tempered by common sense. Quite
apart from the fact that the thought of going into
business on her own frankly terrified her, the thought
of loneliness was even more frightening. Clay had
known that, of course, and as he felt responsible for
her had quite rightly firmly quashed the whole pro-
ject.

The only thing he had not been right about was
who she would be pining for in her loneliness, she
thought miserably, and he was never going to know
that.

She stared at her reflection in the dressing-table
mirror before she went down to breakfast that morn-

ng, and wondered if she would have the courage to
ackle Clay again over her leaving Rimini. Apart
rom Vicky's recovery, nothing else had been accom-
plished as far as her future was concerned, and she
wondered how long it would be before Clay offered
ler the post of companion to Vicky.

During the past week she had sensed an impatience
about him, and his temper had not been what one
might call equable by any means. She also sensed
that his changeable moods had a lot to do with her
refusal to play things his way, and keep herself free
from the plans he had undoubtedly made for her
future.

A sense of helplessness surged through her as these
thoughts went through her mind. It was a case of her
will against his, and she knew only too well whose
was the strongest. She was safe only as long as he
bided his time. She could avoid meeting his eyes and
thereby refusing to fall under their magnetic hold,
but she would be lost if he took her in his arms. Lost
in the magical world of love. She would not be able
to see the future then, or care. The feel of his strong
arms around her would eclipse any worry or doubt
about the future.

With these unhappy thoughts swirling about her
Sheena went down to breakfast, and was surprised to
find Clay sitting at the table drinking coffee. At her
arrival he rose to his feet and directed her attention
to a letter lying beside her place at table, his dark
eyes closely watching her surprised reaction, and
then a slight flush as she recognized Doyle's writing.

With a nonchalance she was far from feeling
Sheena just nodded and sat down at the table, no
attempting to read the letter but pushing it aside fo
future perusal as if it had been a bill she would hav
to settle some time in the future.

Her hands were not quite steady as she accepte
the cup of coffee Clay had poured out for her, an
she wished fervently that he would leave her to finisl
her breakfast in peace. There was no hope of readin,
the letter until she was back in her bedroom and wa
assured of some privacy, and she bewailed the fac
that she had no pockets on either the blouse or th
jeans she was wearing and could not tuck the lette
away out of sight.

The uppermost thought in her mind was hov
Doyle had got to know her address. She had sen
Cookie a letter about a fortnight ago, but had en
closed the letter in a catalogue envelope that onl
bore the firm's name on it, making certain that th
letter would arouse no suspicion from Doyle whe
sorted through the mail each morning. In any case
Cookie did not know her full address, so the informa
tion had not come from her.

'Would that be the hoped-for reconciliation?
asked Clay softly, his eyes on the letter that Sheen;
was trying to ignore as she settled down to eat th
breakfast that Pietro had brought in for her on he
arrival.

Sheena's eyes left her food, and she put down he
knife and fork, abandoning any hope of finishing th
meal. Whatever appetite she had was now completel
gone.

As she sought for some cutting answer that would tell Clay that she had no intention of discussing such subject, she vaguely wondered where Vicky was. Vicky did not miss meals, her healthy appetite assured this. No sooner than the thought was there, so was the answer! Clay had given her her marching orders, and this must have included Pietro, she thought dully, as he was usually in and out of the kitchen during meal times, either taking away the used plates or replenishing the coffee pot, but he had not appeared again after bringing her her breakfast.

Clay had known that the letter was from Doyle, but how? How had he known? Her eyes widened as the horrible thought struck her that he might have read the letter, and it was all that she could do not to snatch it up and assure herself that it had not been opened.

With her eyes on Clay she said, 'How did he get my address?' She knew the answer before he verified it. Clay had given it to him. She swallowed. He hadn't known what to do with her. He must have got tired of waiting for her to fall in with his plans, and suddenly decided that they weren't worth carrying on with.

He must, she thought frantically, now be pinning his hopes on Doyle coming good, and taking her off his hands.

Even though she knew the answer, it still shocked her to hear Clay say, 'I sent it to him—at least,' he mended casually, 'I enclosed your letter to your friend in one of the farm's envelopes, and re-addressed it.'

Sheena couldn't bear to look at him as she asked 'Why?' in a low voice. She knew the answer would hurt her more than anything had ever hurt her before even after what had happened with her father, but she had to hear him say it.

'Because I've come to the end of the line with you,' he said harshly. 'I would have been content to give you more time, but it wouldn't solve anything, would it?' He stared at the letter. 'You might,' he said grimly, 'just confirm that I'm right in assuming that Charter wants you back, but no way,' he added harshly, 'will you be going back unless he makes you a firm offer of marriage.'

Sheena's eyes blazed at this autocratic ruling. How dared he? What did he care whether she married Doyle or not? He might feel responsible for her, but there were limits! All he was really interested in was getting her off his hands! 'I think I'm old enough to make my own decisions,' she said quietly, but as the fury bubbled up within her she added furiously, 'What right have you to lay any conditions on my return, anyway?'

'The right of someone who cares deeply for you,' he replied. His eyes were bleak as he continued 'Who loves you enough to let you go back to the one person who can make you happy.'

Sheena's stupefied expression said it all. There was so much she wanted to know, and she was not certain that she had heard what she thought she had heard. 'I'm not going back to Barter's Ridge,' was all she could think of saying, but she couldn't leave it at that. If Clay loved her, then why was he standing the other side of the table just looking at her? 'Do you really love me?' she asked in a small wondering voice.

Still he did not move towards her, but gave her a tight-lipped smile. 'I've been telling you so since that first day,' he said quietly. 'But you kept blocking me out. I couldn't even get off the starting line, let alone make you forget Charter.'

Sheena's wondering eyes swept over Clay's proud head, and his strongly moulded jaw, and on to those firm lips of his. He didn't know it, but he had succeeded in his quest within a week of her arrival. The night of the dance, she thought dreamily. It had only taken one kiss, that was all, to awaken her from her dreaming.

'Why aren't you going back?' he shot out at her, shaking her out of her misty musings. 'Do you find it hard to forgive him, too? Will you spend the rest of your life with only memories to comfort you?' he said harshly.

Sheena gazed steadily back at him and slowly shook her head, making her dark hair frame her heart-shaped face.

'Then why, Sheena?' he asked persistently, the strain evident by his taut expression.

'If a certain person would only take me in his arms and kiss me, I think——'

That was as far as Clay allowed her to get, and the next minute he was holding her tight in his arms and kissing her with a ferocity that left no room for doubt that he loved her. 'I'll kiss you through to eternity,' he whispered against her lips, 'because I'll never let you go. I'll forge a chain of love around you that will bind you to me for the rest of time.'

Through the pink haze of love Sheena reflected that the chain was already there, he had no need of reinforcement. She felt his hold slacken on her and knew he was reaching for the letter on the table behind her. He held it in front of her for a brief second, then crushed it in his strong lean hand. 'Exit one station boss,' he said softly, then swept her close to him again, 'and here's where the farm boss takes over!'